Also by M.A. Wakefield

The Dreaming Fields, Volume 1: The Magic of Science

The Dreaming Fields

Volume II

THE
Science
of MAGIC

M.A. Wakefield

the **Science**
of **Magic**

The Dreaming Fields
Volume II

No part of this book may be used or reproduced by any means, graphic, electronic, or mechanical, including photocopying, recording, taping or by any information storage retrieval system without the written permission of the publisher except in the case of brief quotations embodied in critical articles and reviews.

ISBN: 978-1-63760-219-5 [paperback]
ISBN: 978-1-63795-266-5 [e-book]

book design | m.a. wakefield | | cover illustration | shutterstock.com

*For the Dreamers,
and the Dreamed.*

Chapter 1

THE CAMP lay in smoldering ruins, bunker entrances gaping like empty sockets in a rotting skull. From a few of them, wisps of smoke were still rising, dissipating into the bright afternoon. Between the bunkers and the tree-line that marked the river's edge, the sleepy meadow had been churned into a swath of clumped and broken mud-holes that suggested many soldiers and much machinery.

With a heavy heart, Milos picked his way down the hillside. Four or five trees lay with their roots pointed at the sky, their splintered trunks like broken toothpicks. Shreds of bark and wood littered the hillside and meadow below.

Maia has been taken.

This thought pained him, but he spent no time on remorse – he could only move forward now.

An ominous feeling had plagued him for most of the previous day, and as twilight had come to the hidden house he shared with the others in the high mountains, he'd slipped alone toward the valley below, his uneasiness turning to dreadful certainty the further he went.

He'd heard the helicopters as they came down the valley, had witnessed most of the horror from a hidden spot on the north side of the river, sitting motionless on the limb of a huge oak that dominated the tree-spotted riverbank, opposite the meadow.

The sadness, the sense of loss as he witnessed the slaughter, was overwhelming. Even with his prodigious emotional control, it was all he could do to remain hidden when everything inside him wanted to break cover and try to help. But the damage had already been done; there was nothing one man could do, even if that man was a sorcerer.

There was nothing to do but wait and watch...and try to locate Maia.

If she's still alive.

He ignored this pessimistic thought; he was certain, in some way that defied explanation, that she hadn't been killed in the initial attack. He could feel her in the forest.

Even so, it took a supreme effort to clear his mind enough to use his dreaming body. Somehow, he managed it; his consciousness rose out of his inert body, hovering over the water and tuned to the night.

He found her only moments later, moving furtively up-valley. He was about to try to contact her - another bit of magic that would have required all his skill and concentration - but before he could, a new element of his vision caused him to snap awake with such force that he over-balanced and fell from the low branch, crashing into a nest of moldy bracken and scraping skin from his elbows. He barely noticed the pain, though; what he'd seen had been strange enough to override all other thoughts. Even the slaughter on the other side of the river was momentarily forgotten.

This can't be! It simply can't!

He leapt to his feet, feeling a sudden surge of energy, and made his way up-valley as quickly as he could, towards Maia and her desperate escape with the companion who'd sparked his sudden alarm. He tried to stay under cover, but in his excitement, it was hard not to run.

He tried to compensate for the differences between his dreamtime vision and the waking world, but he still over-shot the area he was looking for, then wasted half an hour backtracking around an impassable blackberry thicket that covered at least a ten-acre area.

By the time he'd physically located Maia and her strange companion, the main compound was far behind, the night thick and dark. He shadowed them, trying to keep them in sight while navigating the steep, tricky terrain on the north side of the river. There were no paths, and more than once he had to let his dreaming body take over for a few minutes to find them again.

The dawn was painting the forest in shades of silver and gold as finally, exhausted, he climbed the stair-step boulders to the top of the falls, resting for a moment as he shaded his eyes and looked for movement below.

A moment later, he saw them as they broke out of the trees, onto the cracked plain below. Again, his heart quickened as he beheld her companion – the same young man she'd been with that day.

The one who was abducted.

The fact of the young man's reappearance was not the source of Milos' sudden excitement, however. Once again, he wondered at the extreme improbability of what he was seeing.

What he's doing is impossible! How is he accomplishing it?

He watched them for a few minutes, using all his skills to see Johnny's energy carefully, making certain he was correct in his assessment.

Martuk will want to know about this immediately.

He thought of trying to contact his benefactor remotely - Martuk, an adept of the dreaming fields, wouldn't be hard to find with his dreaming body - and was about to make the attempt when a movement from the cracked plain below caught his attention. Alarmed, he sprang to his feet, muscles tensed, ready to run to Maia's aid...

But it was already too late; once again he could do nothing but watch, angry and frustrated, as the troopers advanced. And, in some ways, this was even worse than what he'd witnessed earlier.

Maia represented much more than an investment of time; she was more than just a student, or even a friend. Her presence was absolutely vital to the plans he'd laid with Martuk and the others; plans for a true sorcerer's journey, one that he'd seen many times over in his dreams. But there was no margin for error. In order to achieve this journey, not only must the sorcerers' combined intent be flawless, but their configuration must be complete.

If Maia is lost, then so are we all.

A pang of hopelessness passed through him, but he let it go, keeping himself attuned to the moment as his training mandated...and so it happened that he witnessed a very strange thing, a thing neither Maia nor the firing soldiers could see from atop the cliff.

Johnny Perdue had not fallen to his death from the arid cliff-top.

Overwhelmed by numbers and firepower, he was finally blasted from the precipice. His body arced out, falling much too slowly through the sparkling, empty space above the pool, and then...

And then he'd dissipated; that is, he'd come apart as if he had no more substance than smoke, and then simply disappeared, literally into thin air.

Based on what Milos had already seen, he wasn't completely caught off guard...but still, it was a strange and frightening omen. Casting a last look at

Maia – trussed up, laid out on a white gurney and being wheeled toward a waiting helicopter – he turned and struck into the forest.

He found his way up the steep, hidden trail that led to the higher mountains where he lived with Martuk and the others, and by midday he was home.

He'd wasted no time in apprising them all of the situation. By the time dusk brought shadows to their doorstep, a plan of action had been formed.

Milos had come down to the valley early this morning, taking his leave of Martuk and the others before daybreak. They were traveling even now, heading west towards the coast and Maia, and he planned to catch up with them before nightfall...but this morning, he was on a unique mission, one that promised to be as challenging as it was strange.

He spent an hour or so sitting on a large rock in the cold sun, examining his memories of Johnny Perdue, and when he felt he had what was needed, he got to his feet and began walking down-valley, following the river.

CHAPTER 2

JOHNNY PERDUE couldn't remember how long he'd been walking, but he thought it was a very long time.

He was in the forest, down-valley from Compound West, near the Knob...or at least he thought so. This information swam up from the depths, seemingly of its own accord. He stopped to orient himself, looking his body over as if for the first time.

He was clad in a rough blue homespun shirt and faded jeans. On his feet were his familiar, cracked black leather boots. Lifting one foot, he brought it down and crushed a twig beneath his heel. Pungent pine wafted to his nostrils.

Well, that's good. I appear to actually be *here.*

Unsure of what this thought might mean, he nevertheless began walking toward where the compound should be, perhaps only a bit more than a quarter mile up-valley.

He moved with sure, confident strides at first, but as he progressed, a vague dread began to overtake him. He found himself walking more and more slowly despite his best intent, his brow furrowed in concentration as he tried to figure it out...tried to remember...what?

Something bad happened here.

There was no rational basis for this thought, no accompanying memories, but he felt it was true, just the same.

He remembered nothing that had transpired since the day he'd gone to the Falls with Maia, and his memories from before that day, though mostly clear, were distant, as if they'd happened to someone else.

Those things did *happen to someone else. Whoever I was, I'm different now.*

Other, more recent memories seemed to be there too, flitting like shadows in his imagination...but when he turned a probing eye on them, they wavered and disappeared like so much vapor.

Still...the compound. Something happened.

As he crested the low rise of the Knob and caught his first view of the trashed remains of his home, he felt that his heart had stopped. For a seeming eternity he could only stand there, swaying and stunned, as he beheld the empty, gaping eyes of the bunker entrances.

Dead...all dead. No one survived this.

Feeling utterly drained, he sat with his back against a tree, his mind spinning out of control, looking for memories and connections where none could be found.

Maia...she's gone, too.

Numb, horrified, but too exhausted to move or think, he simply sat there as the sun moved toward the roof of the sky, transforming morning into midday.

And, no matter how he tried to stop it, his wayward mind continued on its harried pace, searching for memories and connections, trying to put the puzzle together. Images chased each other across his mind's eye; Compound life, the Control bunker, the Aldridges...Karla...Maia...

After a while he found his feet again, and moved slowly toward the smoking wreckage that had been his life.

He wandered numbly through the remains for an hour or more, always expecting to hear voices, to see someone (anyone!) step out from behind a tree and hail him...but no one did.

Compound West is really gone.

He entered the kitchen bunker and found it utterly empty - even the tables and chairs were gone. It appeared that the place had been summarily cleaned out, down to personal items and foodstuffs.

He wandered outside, making his way along the base of the hill to a familiar entrance – the one leading to the rooms he'd shared recently with Maia and the Aldridge family. A charred, unpleasant smell greeted him, and he paused before entering.

That's the smell of death.

The bunkers were lifeless holes. Everything had been removed, just as in the kitchen. He didn't stay there long – the atmosphere was so morose, so utterly dreadful that he couldn't take very much of it.

He didn't visit any more of the bunkers, with the exception of Control; he thought there was an outside chance it might have escaped detection. And though he didn't believe for a second that this was the case, a sense of duty compelled him to make sure.

The door to the Control room – the place he'd worked, with John Stark and Marshall Scott, to keep the compound secure – had been blown off its hinges, and there were multiple blackened, charred holes in the wall, evidence of an altercation.

Somebody put up a fight – Stark or Scott, I'm sure. I hope they took some of the bastards with 'em.

But this room was as empty as all the others, and he made his way back outside quickly, feeling almost dizzy by the time he was in the sunlight again.

I hope they were able to wipe the computers before they were taken.

He knew there had been a self-destruct program in place, a digital bomb designed by John Stark to wipe the computers clean in case of just this sort of event...

But did they have time to run it?

This thought made him queasy, and he tried to push it away. If the computers had been taken with their memories intact, then the other four North American compounds were all in grave danger.

Johnny tried not to think of his friends in Montana, and what it would mean if records of their existence had been found here.

There's nothing I can do.

The sun was well past its zenith now, the afternoon moving steadily along. Not really thinking about where he was going, he made his way back to the wide meadow that lay between the bunkers and the riverbank. He was compelled by a craving for solace; a need for light, and open space, and time to think in the sunshine.

*****

Near the riverbank at the upper end of the meadow, he found something he hadn't seen on his way to Control; a patch of freshly moved dirt, perhaps twenty yards by ten, slightly mounded. Nearby, wisps of smoke still escaped from the remains of a large bonfire, reduced now to nothing but charcoal and ash.

He was momentarily puzzled, but understanding came quickly enough, roaring in with his anger, a great tide of fire that swept his mind clean. His cry, when it came, was choked and strangled.

"Oh, you unholy BASTARDS!"

His friends had been gunned down like rats in their nests, then buried here; plowed under and relegated to this mass, unmarked grave, all their worldly possessions reduced to so much ash.

Discarded, like junk.

Shaking with numb rage, he cast about on the slope, littered with the crushed remains of local plant life. When he found what he wanted – a medium-large granite boulder with one flat side – he picked it up and carried it to the far end of the humped mass of freshly packed earth.

His next search took a little longer, but soon he'd found a small, jagged chunk of obsidian that would do the trick. He began working, marking the flat side of the boulder with it, scratching only two words deeply into the face of the granite. The script was rough, and he knew that time and weather would smooth the words before too many years had passed...but it would have to do.

He stepped back to survey his work, and was overtaken suddenly with alien emotion. An indescribable sadness welled from deep within; a nerve-shattering resonance of piercing, heart-rending dissonance that tore from him all vestige of sanity. Growling like an animal, he clapped his hands to his head, tearing at his hair. He pounded fists into his forehead and temples, scratching at his cheeks, biting down as hard as he could on his lips, and the insides of his cheeks.

And felt no pain whatsoever. No blood flowed, no matter how hard he tried. He clenched his fists and ground his teeth, his whole being fairly vibrating with impotent rage.

I need to cry! I need to let this out!

But though the rage and sorrow continued to build, he remained dry-eyed.

Mindless with grief, he began to pick up stones, hurling them with terrible, deadly focus at the trees on the hillside, trying to scream out this terrible feeling with feral, wordless shrieks. A rock the size of a man's fist smashed through a nearby shrub, sending a shower of leaves to the earth. Another banged off the trunk of a tall pine with enough force to leave a fresh white scar in the bark. A volley of stone missiles sent chipmunks racing for cover, and a flock of crows screamed in protest as they took to the air in a storm of black wings.

With a final strangled roar, he picked up a chunk of granite the size of a cow's head and rocketed it, one-handed, at a bare white birch fifty feet up the hillside. It flew like a cannonball and struck the bole of the tree dead-center, snapping it cleanly in half with an ear-splitting *craaaaaack!* as if it were nothing but a matchstick.

Exhausted, he collapsed beside the gravestone he'd fashioned, and read as if in a trance the words he'd written there:

'THEY LIVED'

*****

Silence ruled the day; nothing moved in the forest.

The afternoon was half gone, and with an unsettling shiver, it occurred to Johnny for the first time that he really had no idea which way he should go, or what he hoped to find. A cloistering, humid feeling seemed to come from the very air around; overhead, the sky was gray static, and an empty wind sighed forlornly among the skeletons of the trees.

Panic began to threaten, and with it despair.

What should I do? What can I do?

Thoroughly unexpected, a voice came from the silence.

"Good afternoon, Johnny Perdue."

A surge of fear propelled him to his feet, and he looked wildly around for a moment before he spotted the speaker: a man of some indistinct age, perhaps between thirty-five and sixty, with shoulder-length brown hair and blunt features. He had a wide jaw and cheekbones, and large dark eyes that peered from beneath a wide-brimmed hat. The man put both hands on his hips and laughed; a rich, friendly sound.

"I'm sorry to startle you, Johnny. Allow me to properly introduce myself." He swept his hat off with a theatrical bow, his amused eyes never leaving Johnny's. "My name is Milos, and I am at your service."

Strange. Why does he seem so familiar?

Johnny frowned, trying to think, but couldn't quite put his finger on it. Questions flooded his mind as he gaped at the newcomer.

"How do you know my name?" He blurted finally.

Milos smiled and sat down cross-legged in the grass. "I am...well, I guess you'd say that I'm Maia's friend." Johnny found the man's eyes soothing, and strangely active...as if his gaze were a live thing, commanding a force all its own. "Actually," Milos continued, "It would be more accurate to say that I'm her teacher...but now I'm getting ahead of myself."

Johnny's thoughts were a confused muddle.

"But Maia...she never mentioned...I mean, how? And anyway...well, she's...she's gone, man." He indicated the mass grave. "They're all gone."

Milos shook his head firmly, eyes sparkling.

"She's alive, Johnny. Don't you remember? You were with her, on the upper plain, just below the Falls. It was only yesterday morning, after all."

Milos' words seemed to rearrange something in Johnny's memory. He saw her in his mind's eye suddenly, her hair reflecting the morning sunlight, the Falls in the background...and the troopers, advancing across the plain.

"They...they took her." Johnny's face was a mask of stone, his eyes flat. His voice was soft and even. "But how could you know that? Who *are* you?"

"I saw it happen," Milos said quietly. "When I learned that your compound was under attack, I came immediately. I waited all night for an opportunity to get her away safely, but unfortunately, that opportunity never arrived. I was about to make my move when the soldiers came." His face tightened into a momentary grimace. "There's only so much one man can do. But she is alive, Johnny. You can count on that. And we're going after her."

"We? You mean you and I?" Hope bloomed, unexpected and welcome.

"You and I, and a few of my – and Maia's – friends. They're camped below the foot of the valley, only a few miles from here. I'm on my way to meet them now - I only came this way to see if I could find you." He smiled. "And wouldn't you know it. Lucky me."

Johnny was intrigued. "To find me?"

"That's right." Milos studied him with calm, penetrating eyes. "Can I ask you a question, Johnny?"

"Sure."

"Where were you, this morning – before you were here, I mean. Can you remember?"

"I was...I was..."

Around them, the forest fell to a ghostly hush, as if the creatures were all watching, waiting expectantly. Johnny felt a chill run the length of his spine. "I don't know," he said after a moment. "I can't remember."

Milos nodded. "Exactly as I thought," he said. "Well, wherever you were, it's no accident that you're here now." He looked at Johnny meaningfully.

"Are you saying..." Johnny frowned, trying to understand. "Are you saying that you...brought me here? That you summoned me, like some sort of djinn?"

Milos got to his feet with startling speed. His eyes burned from within as he gripped Johnny's shoulder. "You must come with me," he said decisively. "We might need your help...but you most certainly need ours."

Under normal conditions, Johnny would have been wary, even paranoid, at such a proposition, especially considering how the fellow had so deftly put aside his question. Instead, he realized with some surprise that Milos' presence seemed to be galvanizing him somehow...strengthening him.

"All right," he heard himself say.

Milos smiled widely. "Good! It's settled, then. Follow me if you're ready."

CHAPTER 3

CONSCIOUSNESS CAME SLOWLY, lifting Maia like a raft on the swell of a spring flood, bearing her over swollen, troubled waters toward the gray light of a day that didn't want to be born.

Visions skittered across the tortured, stormy surface of her mind's eye, waking-up dreams that seemed somehow too vivid to be real.

Again and again she saw him, blasted and falling, his face haloed by orange light, eyes wide, mouthing her name. Again and again she reached for him, and each time he was only an arm's length, a finger's length, a hair's width away. And each time she failed to save him.

Her eyes tried to blink open and found a world of sterile gray indifference, alien and cold.

There was no apparent pain, which was something. Lying with her eyes closed to slits, she wiggled the toes of her right foot, then her left. Everything seemed to be functioning. She repeated the process with her arms and hands and was relieved to find that all was in working order.

She took a deep breath, tasting warm air that seemed somehow both fresh and stale, then exhaled slowly, relishing the sensation. Screwing up her courage, she drew in another breath and opened her eyes all the way.

She was indoors, no question about that. A low white ceiling dominated her vision. It was segmented into perfect squares a few inches wide. Looking at it for more than a moment made her feel dizzy, so she sat up.

The room was smallish, but not cramped, and lit with soft, hidden fluorescent lights that nestled into the exacting right angles between walls and ceiling. She was on a mattress, set low to the floor and just big enough for her to lie on comfortably. It was covered with a heavy olive-green blanket made of some slick material that she didn't much care for.

The first thing she noticed was the lack of color. The room was frightfully austere - there were no windows, just the bed, a small table next to it, and two doors. On the wall adjacent to the foot of the bed was a screen – she recognized it as being akin to the old computer monitors that Stark and Scott had cobbled together in Control. But this one was different – it was nearly paper-thin and stuck to the center of the wall like a square gray metallic pool, gazing at her with reflective coldness. She could see herself in it, a tiny figure with mussed hair and large, scared eyes, dressed in plain gray pants and a white shirt that felt weird against her skin. The reflection threatened to carry her away, and she shivered and squeezed her eyes tight.

I have to focus.

Panic began to threaten. To fight it, she got up and began to examine every detail of her surroundings, though there wasn't much detail to begin with.

The first door was locked; the second stood slightly ajar, and upon a moment's inspection proved to be that of a small lavatory.

For a moment she stood staring, taking in this strange room. She had never seen a toilet before, though she recognized it from pictures she'd seen, and comprehended its purpose immediately. The shower stall was a greater mystery, and it took a few minutes of experimentation to figure out what it was for. Imagine! The luxury of washing yourself for as long as you wanted, with water that was exactly the right temperature. Even though she was frightened nearly out of her wits, she was a curious person by nature, and the only thing that kept her from trying it was the thought of removing all of her clothes. Something about the screen on the wall seemed to sound an inner alarm. Wherever she was, she felt that it likely that the people who had kidnapped her were watching her, perhaps even at this very moment.

This thought was horribly frightening. She shut the door to the small lavatory and paced the circumference of the room again, hands clasped tightly across her stomach. She returned to the bed and sat on it, trying to calm her accelerated breathing. She took several deep breaths and began her internal mantra.

✻✻✻✻✻

I am a child of the universe...

The panic begins to leave as the lungs fill with air. The body begins to be aware of light, and

I am a being of light...

the room comes into focus. Even in this room, with no color and no windows, there is light, and

the power of light is the power of love...

where there is light, there is the potential for love. The heartbeat begins to slow, to become a regular clockwork again, *tick-tock, tick-tock,* and she remembers that she has

the power of love is the power of life...

the power to change her circumstances, to affect her surroundings by the pure light of her

life is the essence of the universe...

life. She doesn't know how she knows this, but the mantra

i am a child of the universe...

continues, bringing her to center, expanding her consciousness so that even this place, this apparent prison, can be a source of peace and understanding. Deep in her memory, something turns over uneasily and a name

Milos

rises to the surface of her awareness, along with an image – a face with calm dark eyes in a wide face.

I am a child of the universe...

✻✻✻✻✻

For no good reason, she rose suddenly and returned to the first, locked door. For a moment she only stood in front of it, feeling a bit stupid but convinced that maybe she could open it with the force of her will alone. It was an alien feeling, a deep and exciting itch in the center of her abdomen, somehow connected to that name

Milos

that she knew but couldn't place. She focused her energy on the doorknob. For a second she was convinced that it would turn, that she could open it...

There was a sudden knock on the door. She let out an involuntary, breathless scream, and then the door swung open to reveal a young man in a silver singlesuit.

His eyes were unthreatening; he seemed almost wary. "Hello," he said. "I'm..." An odd, tortured look passed across his face. "I'm s-s-sorry," he stuttered. "I didn't mean to scare you."

"It's all right." She had her breath back now and looked at him warily, clasping her arms across her chest in a posture of nervous defensiveness.

He looked around seventeen or eighteen years old, but there was something about him that set him apart from other adolescent youths she had known. His face was smooth and boyish, yet he was well-muscled, as if he'd spent years working on his physique. His head seemed a little too big for his body, as well, but it was mostly his eyes that gave away the secret. The mind that lurked behind those eyes couldn't possibly be that of a normal adolescent. There was too much there, and at the same time not nearly enough. She couldn't have explained it rationally, but she knew there was something very odd about him. Those eyes spoke of untold knowledge and teeth-gnashing fear dreams, and yet they were the guile-less eyes of a child, filled with a child's fears and hopes.

They reminded her, oddly, of Karla's eyes.

"I'm Daniel," he said, and stepped aside with a small bow so that she could see the sparsely furnished yet quietly plush apartment beyond. "I'm at your service, as much as I can be. Would you like to see the rest of your quarters?"

✳✳✳✳✳

The main room of the condo was sparsely furnished and perhaps twice the size of the bedroom where she had awakened. A low sofa relaxed against one wall, bookended by a pair of small end-tables. On these stood a matched pair of tan and green lamps, glowing with friendly yellow light.

The rich green carpet covering the floor from wall to wall was plush but firm and felt good under her feet. On the walls were two framed paintings, both abstract prints that made great use of various shades of purple and green. These she didn't much care for.

At one end of the room was a short hallway; beyond that was a door. The door was shut, but she assumed that it was the door the young man had used to get into this room.

That one goes Outside.

"I had to pull a few strings, but I was able to get you a room with a view," Daniel said. "Look, over here."

He walked to the other end of the room and pulled aside a heavy, old-fashioned curtain.   The room was flooded with light; real light, natural daylight. For a moment, Maia squinted against the unexpected glare, holding up a hand to shade her face.

When her eyes had adjusted, she looked out from an unexpected height over a vast, pristinely manicured lawn. Dozens of varieties of flowers filled the scene with their muted colors, giving the whole thing the feel of a watercolor painting.

A few hundred yards away, the landscape ended abruptly at a precipice, and beyond this was the ocean.

Her heart nearly stopped at the sight. White and gray gulls soared and swooped above waves of sparkling blue that stretched to the horizon. The sun was molten gold, low above the water, sending distorted tracers of color running back towards her.

She touched the glass and was amazed to discover that it was a door, not a window.   Outside was a spacious deck with a wooden rail, a few scattered potted plants, and two low-slung chairs of some comfortable-looking material.

"I thought you might like this room," Daniel said, and there was a note of satisfaction in his voice. And something else, as well; not jealousy, or greed, but some combination of the two that she couldn't quite name.

He reached past her and flicked the catch on the glass door, then slid it open. It moved silently on hidden, well-oiled tracks, and the sounds of the afternoon flooded in, filling her with a combination of joy and sadness so unexpectedly fierce that she found herself suddenly crying. She wrapped her arms around herself and turned away from him, raising her face to the sky, weeping silently.

When she turned back toward him, her face was tear-streaked, but her eyes blazed.

"Who are you people?!" She pointed the words at him like a loaded gun, compacting all the considerable force of her personality into one sentence. He stepped back an uneasy pace, guilt and concern warring with that other, unnamed emotion on his wide, smooth face.

Possessiveness, intuition whispered. *He wants to* own *you.*

"Please!" He raised his hands in a defensive gesture. "Please, I understand why you're upset, but let me explain." He hesitated, bit his lip. A troubled look played across his odd features.

"Maybe we should sit down," he ventured after a moment. "I...what is your name? Will you tell me that?"

She crossed the deck to one of the chairs, unmindful of the nipping wind, and sat down heavily. She wanted to remain angry, indignant, but she was also curious...and mindful of her predicament. It wouldn't do to fly off the handle at this young man, who likely had nothing to do with what had happened at Compound West.

"Maia," she said, offering what she hoped was a grateful smile, trying to erase all traces of anger from her voice. "My name's Maia."

She sat back into the reclining deck chair, trying to appear relaxed, remaining alert. Later, when this strange young man had gone away, she would cry for her friends, and for Johnny, and for herself...but for now, information was key. She must find out as much as she could, must even strive to befriend him if it seemed possible.

His face was troubled. He stood awkwardly, one hand on the rail, looking out at the sea. After a moment, he seemed to remember that he'd asked her to sit, and took the chair next to her with an oddly swift motion. He sat very still for a moment, leaning forward, hands clasped between his knees. Maia was struck with the odd realization that he was at least as scared and nervous as she. She found this thought absurd, and laughed despite herself.

He looked up at her, eyes betraying his turmoil. He bit the inside of his lip and studied her gravely.

She covered her mouth to stifle her giggle. "I'm sorry," she said. "I didn't mean to...I mean..."

"It's quite all right," he said quietly. "If anything, I should be apologizing to you." He stared out at the lowering sun, frowning in thought.

"I'm Daniel," he said again, though she hadn't forgotten his name. "I'm not quite sure where to begin."

"Maybe you could tell me what I'm doing here, and why my friends and family have been killed." Her voice was far more calm than she felt.

His face clouded. "Well, that's a fair question," he said. "Although I probably can't give you a satisfactory answer. The best I could do is to tell you that you are the victim of a system that is accustomed to using people like tools to achieve its ends." He sighed. "In some ways, you and I aren't that different."

"Hmmm." She bit back an angry retort, smoothed her mind, assimilated information. "How do you mean?"

His face took on that tortured look again. When he spoke, it was in furtive tones. He glanced around as if afraid he was being watched. "I...well, let's just say that I know what it's like to feel like you are out of choices. Like you're only a pawn in a giant game of chess."

Maia, who had never once in her life felt that way, raised her eyebrows in silent question.

He went on, hands clasping and unclasping between his knees. "I...that is, my grandfather is a...well, a powerful man, I guess you would say. He represents people whose interests span the globe. I guess you could say that he's like a police chief."

She smiled, comprehending the concept although inexperienced with its practicalities. "Go on, please."

"He's been training me to follow in his footsteps. I am to be initiated into the Brotherhood in less than two weeks." He looked up at her, eyes somehow pleading and arrogant at the same time. "I am the youngest ever to achieve such an honor."

She smiled demurely, masking her shocked fascination with this young man. There was something so dual, so *other* about him – ancient evil and unchecked infantilism stitched together with adolescent insecurity into a constantly shifting patchwork personality. "That's very nice," she said. "But where do I come into this picture?"

"Right. I'm getting to that." He gazed at her sidelong. "I....I must admit that you were spared because of me," he said. "I..." his throat worked, up and down, but no sound came out for almost a minute. Twice Maia started to say something, then changed her mind. Whatever was to happen, she felt that Daniel would divulge more information if she just allowed him to talk.

When he spoke, his voice was so low that it was nearly drowned by the distant crash of the waves and the cries of the gulls, brought on the soft evening breeze. Maia sat up straighter in her chair, listening intently.

"I couldn't let it happen to you," he said. "I...I saw you. On surveillance. You..." His throat worked again, cheeks blooming red as he fought for control. He pushed through his hesitancy, rushing through the next sentence almost angrily.

"You're beautiful!" he exclaimed. "You're the most beautiful woman I've ever seen, and I couldn't let you die. There's just something about you, I guess.

I don't know what it is, but when I saw you..." He raised his arms in the universal gesture of helplessness, letting his sentence trail off.

A cold revulsion turned Maia's stomach to stone, and she quelled her outrage only with substantial effort. "So...so you've been watching us, then? You've been watching *me*? And you saved me because you find me beautiful?! What about my friends? Were they too ugly? Was that why they died?"

He flushed again, but set his jaw and looked her in the eyes anyway. "You have to understand that I didn't want any of this to happen," he said, speaking so quietly that she strained to hear his words. "I never believed that your group was a terrorist faction, but that decision was never mine to make. Like I said, I know what it's like to –"

"Terrorist faction?" She laughed, a ragged, angry sound that caught in her throat and made her feel like screaming. "That's what you believe?"

"No!" His eyes were bright and agonized. "No, I told you, I never..."

But she pushed on, unable (or maybe unwilling) to completely control the anger this time. "Let me tell you something about these *terrorists*," she snapped. "These were mothers and fathers, and innocent children! These people wanted nothing more than to go about their lives in peace!" Her voice was raised to breaking pitch, blood flaming in her cheeks, and he stared at her wide-eyed and surprised.

She sat back, breathing heavily but trying not to show it. The cold feeling in the pit of her stomach had turned to steel. She glared at him heavily.

"I'm sorry." His voice was that of a bewildered child, lost and faltering. "I told you...I didn't want it to happen. It wasn't my choice."

Her voice was cold as she replied. "But you had a part in it." She realized it suddenly, as a fact. He'd been unconsciously telling her the whole time. "You killed my friends."

"Well...not me personally." Hands clasped and unclasped, over and over. His face was tortured beyond repair. "But...yes. I guess so." He sighed again, and the sound was so melancholy that she softened, if only a little. "You must understand, if it hadn't been my team, someone else would have done it. The moment your people were spotted, their fate was sealed. It didn't matter who executed the order."

Maia's mind was still, tuned to Daniel's fascinating, ever-changing face. It occurred to her that something beyond the scope of her imagination was happening to her, something she had no context for. And in a sudden burst of knowing, she realized that she was ready for it, had always been ready for it. A clear burst of energy like cool water splashed through her.

Steady, Maia...

His voice...Milos. A flash of his face, clear as day, shimmered in the reflecting pool of her mind's eye.

I do know him! I do!

Memories began to shift and align. She laughed, exhilarated with the rush of memory-self that bore her up like a wave into the setting sun. She rose and walked with sure steps to the rail, setting her face to the breeze that rose from the perfumed gardens below.

"Are you all right?" Daniel seemed unsure of how to respond to her shifting mood. He seemed about to stand, then abruptly sat again.

She let the memory-knowledge pass through her, knowing that she wasn't retaining it all. It was enough to know that Milos was real. Somewhere to the east, she felt him, and laughed again, out loud, at the absurdity.

"I'm fine," she said. "You'll have to excuse me if I'm a little emotional." She turned towards him with a sudden calm resolve. "So what you're really telling me is that I'm lucky," she said, her voice even. "I should have been killed with the others, but you...saved me."

A flash in his eyes confirmed that this was what he wanted her to believe, but he guarded it well. He cleared his throat, looked away.

She took a deep breath and chose her words carefully, laying a gentle hand on his arm as she spoke. "It's all right," she said, knowing that these were the words he wanted to hear from her. "I...appreciate what you've done. It wasn't your fault."

He winced at her touch, as if her hand were very hot or very cold. He lifted his own right hand, very slowly, and reached toward her face, faltering only at the last second. His eyes were full of pain as he lowered his arm, hesitantly. His mouth opened, then closed again, and he shook his head. The heat flush in his cheeks flamed scarlet.

His voice was a choked whisper. "Maia..."

She had a momentary insight – she could own this young man if she wanted, could possess him as fully as he obviously wished to possess her. She could bend him to her will, subvert his mind...

The thought was not without temptation, and she recoiled from it with a violent shiver, horrified by the pleasure she found in such fantasy.

He was watching her intently.

She held his gaze, pushing back at him. "Can you tell me where we are?" she asked, hoping to divert him with a practical question.

He blinked twice, hard, and his posture relaxed. "Uh..." his gaze cleared. "Well, yes, I suppose I can understand you wanting to know that."

He straightened, hands behind his back, and became again the picture of detached professionalism. "We're actually not that far from your former home," he said, not noticing how she winced when he said it. His eyes were far away, as if he was reciting from an internal list. "As you can see, we are situated on the coast. This particular establishment is known as 'Clifftop', for obvious reasons, and is a research and development facility for some of the most promising scientific and military minds of our time."

"I see." Maia wondered if he knew how strange he seemed to her, and decided that he didn't. There was something so obviously wrong about him – the way he seemed to shift between needy little boy and data-brain robot was unnerving.

"As I mentioned," he continued, unaware of how intently she studied him, "you were brought here for...well, let's just say 'personal reasons' and leave it at that. Your friends, the sick little girl and the scientist, are also here, but for very different..." He stopped abruptly, the flow of words shut off like a faucet.

"What?!" Maia's voice was a choked whisper. "What did you say!!?"

His cheeks bloomed again, a more furious shade of brick. "I've said too much. Please, if you value your life, forget what I said." He rose quickly, wringing his hands. "I should go."

"Wait!!" She gripped his forearm, hard. "Please...please, wait." Tears were close, but she fought them back. "If Karla is alive, you must let me see her. You must! She has no one, don't you understand? No one! And neither do I."

Daniel shifted from foot to foot and shook his head, looking quite uncomfortable. "You don't understand," he said slowly. "I don't have that kind of clearance...I mean, I shouldn't have said..."

He looked around desperately as if seeking a way to escape.

She wiped violently at her leaking eyes, suddenly wanting nothing more than to be alone, and simultaneously feeling more lonely than she'd ever felt in her life. She hadn't understood until this very moment just how alone she felt.

Daniel drew a deep breath and looked into her eyes. "I really shouldn't have said anything – it's not my place. But if there's any way to make it happen, I'll try. I..." he hesitated, looking away almost bashfully. "I hate to see you like this...Maia." The way he said her name made her cringe a little, but she held his gaze with a forced smile.

And how exactly did you expect *me to feel?*

"Thank you," she said, hoping her tone held the right notes of gratitude and awe – she knew these were the things he most wanted to see from her, and her survival might well depend on how well she faked them. "Thank you...Daniel."

He pulled back from her, straightening his jacket, and gave her a small bow. "Until next time, then," he said. "If you need anything, select 'SERVICE' on your screen menu or just use the phone and dial zero. I'm sorry to say that it's not within my power to let you roam the grounds, but I may be able to do something about that as well – give me a few days. I'll see you in a day or two, depending on my schedule."

"All right." She was suddenly very fatigued. "Thank you, Daniel."

"You're very welcome." He slid open the glass door and stepped back into the main living area. "Are you sure I can't do anything else for you?"

She sent him what she hoped would be her last fake smile of the afternoon. "I'm fine."

"All right then." His boots thumped through the carpet toward the front door, and then he was gone. The door *snick'd* shut behind him, and Maia was alone with her thoughts and the distant roar of the ocean.

When the tears came, they came freely in a rush, and for a while, sorrow was all she knew.

CHAPTER 4

THEY WALKED QUIETLY for the first hour or so. Johnny found himself growing internally silent by degrees, until it seemed that time had slipped sideways and the only sounds were the restless wind in the grass and trees, the only sight the back of Milos' flat-brimmed hat above his broad shoulders as he led the way.

The valley widened considerably as the sun slipped away, the lowering ridges spreading like open arms on either side as they walked toward the reddening horizon. The grass was tall and green, the evening quiet. They moved in silence, not speaking, feet making hardly a sound. The path was wide and gentle over rolling hills.

Silhouetted in the near distance, a silent V of ducks meandered north, moving across their field of vision in perfect formation, their passage marked by long rows of trees; poplar and oak seemed to equally dominate the landscape as they moved away from the mountains.

They kept the river on their right. It was mostly shallow and broad here, and the weight of the water moved ponderously, like translucent oil. It slid over rounded rocks and under mossy, overhanging limbs, chuckling to itself like a fanatical old man.

As the day slid towards night and twilight deepened, the first stars appeared, lonely and cold, and the sky furred to purple velvet. The lay of the land had evened and flattened out – they walked in a wide meadow of waist-high grass, dotted by the nodding heads of wildflowers. Johnny relished the sensation of free movement through the dusky twilight.

The dreaminess of their surroundings had almost completely lulled him when a sound startled him, and he stopped, listening intently. It was a woman's voice, speaking in a low tone. Someone answered her – a young girl, he thought – and then they both laughed. The sound was inviting but out of place, and he hesitated.

Milos laughed. "Don't worry," he said. "This is my camp." He cupped his hands around his mouth and gave a soft bird-call, which was answered in kind. "Come on," he said. "We're expected."

*****

The encampment was nestled at the washed-out base of a low hillock, beneath the natural semicircle of an earthen wall which gave root to a variety of hardy trees; their entwining branches formed a sort of screen overhead.

A fire crackled merrily in a circle of stones, popping off sparks and swirling smoke. Above the fire, a black iron pot hung suspended, emitting great gouts of steam. A girl of fifteen or so stirred the pot, her slight figure backlit by the orange glow of the flames. A woman sat on a stump nearby, working with something in her hands that was making a dull scraping sound; he couldn't quite make out what it was.

Behind the fire was a tent of rough, stretched canvas over a framework of supple green branches. The front of the tent gaped darkly, but Johnny couldn't see if anyone was inside.

"Hello, Esmerelda," Milos said to the girl stirring the pot.

She looked up. "I'm glad you're back," she said. "I was thinking about coming after you."

He laughed easily as she ladled out a portion of the stew into a wooden bowl and handed it to him. He accepted it and tore off a hunk of bread from a loaf near at hand, eyeing Johnny.

Esmerelda seemed about to offer Johnny some of the food, then hesitated and looked back at Milos, obviously confused about something.

The older man laughed raucously around a mouthful of bread and slurped stew directly from his bowl, eyes never leaving Johnny's. He drained the bowl and delivered a healthy belch, then patted his stomach. "Good stew! You want some, Johnny?"

"I..." Johnny frowned with sudden realization. "I'm not hungry."

It was true. Though he'd been walking most of the afternoon, his body felt energized and light.

"Really? Not hungry at all?" Milos' tone was merry. "Doesn't that strike you as a bit odd?" He lifted his hat, let it fall to his back on its leather cord, then ran a hand through his loose black hair. He replaced the hat firmly and cocked an eyebrow at Johnny. "Never mind, doesn't matter." He waved a hand dismissively.

The woman who'd been sitting on the stump stood up and stepped into the firelight, revealing the large bone-handled knife she'd been sharpening. She sheathed the blade with a fluid, practiced motion.

"Hello, I'm Janet," she said, and then just stood there, looking at him curiously.

She was tall and big-boned. Her face was wide, her features nondescript. Her head was covered by a hat that looked like a smaller version of the one Milos wore. Beneath the flat brim, her eyes burned with steady intelligence in the dancing flame-light.

"Hello," he said. "I'm Johnny." He extended a hand.

She began to lift her own hand to shake with him and then hesitated, looking at Milos with the same expression of confusion Esmerelda had exhibited only moments before.

At this, Milos could contain himself no longer, and broke out in a gale of laughter, slapping his thighs. "Ahhhh, it's too much!" he said. His eyes danced with merriment. "Too much!"

Johnny frowned uncertainly. "What's so funny?" He wanted to get angry but found himself merely curious.

"You'll have to pardon my friends," Milos said. Firelight danced hypnotically from his eyes, across even white teeth. "I told them all about you, but...well, I guess we really didn't know what to expect. You see, although we are all practicing seers, none of us has ever seen anything like you."

A runner of fear snaked through Johnny's midsection. "What do you mean, seers?"

"We are descendants by right of certain ancient traditions," Milos replied. "Our common, abstract goal is total freedom of perception. But I'm getting the cart before the horse. Won't you join me beside the fire?"

Uncertainly, Johnny sat down on a thick, moss-covered log that had been pulled next to the fire. He stretched his hands and feet towards the flames, relishing their radiant warmth.

Milos squatted beside the fire, seeming perfectly comfortable reclining on his haunches. He pushed his hat back on his head and grinned, his dark eyes dancing with humor and good cheer.

Janet retreated to the stump she'd been sitting on when they arrived and went back to sharpening her blade. The sound was somehow comforting. She was a stony wraith, blending perfectly with the darkness – only her eyes were visible beneath the shadow of her hat.

Esmerelda sat on the ground next to Johnny, her back against the moss-covered log. She hugged her knees to her chest, becoming still to the point of nearly blending into the wood. The effect was eerie and unsettling.

The trees whispered; the fire threw sparks; shadows stretched runners into the inky darkness, which had settled in on the camp while no on was looking, a comfortable velvet blanket.

When Milos began to speak, his voice was soft and hypnotic. "We are seers," he began, "as I have already mentioned. The three of us are only a part of our company – Martuk is the eldest and dreams in the shelter yonder..." he motioned toward the makeshift tent, its dark maw gaping and sinister in the half-light. "And Maia – well, of course you know Maia. She's the reason you're here."

Johnny frowned, unconvinced. "If she knows you, then how come she never mentioned you?"

"Maia cannot remember us because she has not tapped the energy at her disposal that would allow her to do so." Milos smiled and shrugged at Johnny's incredulous look. "We are sorcerers," he said, "for lack of a better word. As such, all I can offer is an explanation from within the sorcerer's framework of knowledge."

"But how is that possible?"

Milos fed a handful of small twigs into the guttering flames. "Humans are creatures of perception," he said. "Perceptual engines, if you will. Like all sentient beings, we are here both to create reality and to perceive it. Memories are only layers of perception within the total being."

"A seer sees pure energy," Milos went on. "We have learned to perceive energy in its unadulterated state, to see all things as configurations of energy and all creatures as beings of energy. In a very real way, we perceive the oneness of this world...of all worlds. For there are many worlds, all created from the same basic stuff." He grinned. "Maia could tell you, if she would only remember. She is a true adept of the dreaming fields – a sorceress of dazzling powers. Now, Martuk could really show you, if he—"

"Stop screwing around and tell him the truth about himself." The interrupting voice was old and croaking but somehow powerful.

Milos' smile was broad. "Speak of the devil. Johnny, meet Martuk."

The old man standing just outside his tent looked as if he had been tall once. Now, he was stooped at the shoulders and waist, giving his body a gnarled, twisted look. His face was long and thin, a beak-like nose protruding over a thin-lipped mouth from which most of the teeth seemed to have long since evacuated. Lank white hair fell in wispy lines around his face. He was wrapped in a brick-red blanket that seemed as old as he was, and one bony fist clutched the rounded head of a long, polished walking-stick, his knuckles throwing spidery shadows against the earthen wall behind the tent.

His overall look seemed ancient and decrepit, but his eyes were razor-sharp. They fairly glowed with a blue intensity that was almost difficult to look at. Johnny, full of questions only moments before, found himself nearly hypnotized.

"Hello, young master Perdue," the old man said, hobbling forward into the light of the fire. "I am truly amazed to make your acquaintance...once again." He laughed raucously.

"What do you mean, again? And why would you be amazed to meet me?" Johnny asked. "I think it should be the other way around."

Martuk smiled toothlessly. "Ah, but no!" he exclaimed. "You are a true marvel, my young friend, something I've not seen in all my wanderings." As he spoke, he seemed to change, becoming younger somehow. His body seemed stronger, more there. He spoke with precision and authority. "Milos holds back the truth from you because he wants to control your reaction. He has the interests of a scientist, you see, and to him you represent quite a curiosity. So he sets the stage for his little revelation."

As Martuk spoke, Johnny was amazed and a little horrified to see that the change in the old man's appearance was becoming even more pronounced. He was becoming young before Johnny's astonished eyes. Lank white hair shortened and darkened into deep brown; brittle features became soft and smooth. The stooped back and shoulders straightened out. Martuk smiled widely with a mouth full of even, white teeth, and now Johnny was looking up at a man not yet to middle age, towering over him at a formidable height.

"What...?!" Johnny stared, but Martuk went on, paying him no attention.

"Milos is afraid he might lose you," he said, his voice low and powerful. His eyes gleamed steady blue; with all of the other changes, only they had stayed the same. "He's afraid you won't be able to handle the truth about yourself."

During the course of Martuk's change, the words he was saying had begun to build up an intolerable buzz in Johnny's body. It was as if someone had switched on an electric current in his stomach and was steadily turning it up, one notch every few seconds, until he fairly vibrated with restrained emotion, unfelt thoughts swirling up into consciousness. Memories surfaced, jumbled and garbled but somehow all his; a scrambled totality that was no less total for everything that had happened. Visions flashed by, too fast to grasp.

"What's happening to me?" His voice was a horrified whisper. He was suddenly aware that all four of them were staring at him. "Why are you looking at me like that?" He tried to scream, but all the force had left his voice.

"You're not really there," Janet said, her words methodical and dry.

"You are a dream." Esmerelda's voice was kind but somehow piercing, tearing at layers of repressed feeling surrounding his innermost core. Something fell away and he began to weep silent, dry tears.

"Since Martuk wants to push the issue," Milos said, his voice strangely calm and urgent at the same time, "I will comply. I was almost there, anyhow."

"Good." Martuk sat down abruptly on the log to Esmerelda's left. His body seemed to shrink as he reclined. His features became smooth and waxy, and he assumed the lotus position on the top of the log effortlessly, one leg over the other, somehow holding his balance perfectly. In fact, he looked as if he was actually floating, about an inch above the mossy surface of the log. After a moment, he became so still that he looked like some weirdly lifelike sculpture.

"Who are you people?" Johnny tried to inject some force into his voice, but he was only capable of producing a squeaking whisper.

Martuk's laugh boomed without his changing expression, and the fire glared a brilliant orange for a moment, throwing the scene into ghoulish relief. "The question," he said loudly, face waxen, lips motionless, "is who are you, Johnny Perdue?"

"I was watching for you in the forest today," Milos said. "I went looking for you, as I already told you. What I didn't tell you is that it was likely my presence that determined where and when you re-appeared. Let me ask you this: where were you this afternoon, just before you found yourself walking through the forest? Where did you spend the night?" The seer's eyes were piercing, and Johnny found that he had no answers to the man's questions.

"When you found where they buried your friends, you collected a large rock to use as a gravestone," Milos said. "Do you remember that?"

"Y...yes."

The seer's eyes were sharp. "In your grief, I don't think you even noticed what you were doing...but that boulder must have weighed half a ton. How could you explain such a thing?"

Johnny felt suddenly, incredibly tired. A yawn moved through him, large as the night sky. "Gods, but I'm sleepy," he muttered.

A sudden, expectant quiet fell over the group. Janet raised her eyebrows, addressing Milos with a silent question. From his perch at the end of the log, Martuk's head swiveled eerily until his magnetic blue stare was boring holes in Johnny's head.

"But Johnny, that's what we're trying to tell you," Milos said softly. "You are asleep. You are dreaming."

Johnny woke up enough to laugh derisively. "Great," he said. "So this is all a dream? That's what you're telling me? That's your big revelation?"

Milos' eyes were huge, reflecting the dying embers. "No, you don't understand," he said, his voice soft and even. "This is most definitely not a dream. We are all awake. We are all here, present and accounted for, in our bodies. Only you are dreaming. Your body lies asleep, somewhere far from here, and you are projecting your dreaming body here, to this place."

A wave of disconnected thought smashed through Johnny's mind, and he felt himself beginning to come apart, his body wavering like a mirage. He tried to speak, but could muster no words.

Milos peered at him, seeming to hold him with his eyes. "You are performing a technique that only a veteran sorcerer can perform, Johnny. And not only that, you are performing it perfectly and continuously and have no idea that you're doing it at all. How very strange! In fact, your dreaming body is such a perfect replica of your physical body that you were able to live in this state, at the compound, for nearly two months without anyone having the faintest clue as to what was really going on."

Johnny began to experience a terrible vertigo; Milos' words seemed to bring about a strange chain reaction in him. Inner doors began to creak open, and suddenly he felt too light, as if he might just float away.

"Wait." His voice was faint, shimmering. "Wait a minute. Where did you say my body is?"

A loud cackle of laughter brought him back. It was Martuk, now standing by the fire, hands clasped around the head of his walking stick. He was again a stooped, toothless old man. His eyes were burning blue, reflecting the suddenly bright flames. "Don't go to sleep, Johnny," he croaked. "You never know where you might wake up."

"I don't know where your body is," Milos went on calmly, ignoring them both. "But I think it might be somewhere underground."

"Underground?" Johnny's voice seemed faint in his own ears.

"The day you and Maia went to the falls – the day you took the seer's fungus – I was there. I was above the waterfall and saw the two of you below. I wanted to talk to Maia, but you were there, and that complicated things. I was wondering if I might be able to pull her aside without you noticing, because the two of you were both in a mildly hallucinogenic state. But then I noticed them."

"Them?"

"I still don't know what they are," Milos said. "All I know is that they are psychically much more powerful than the average human. They were shielding themselves somehow, so they were virtually invisible to the naked eye. I could only perceive them in the manner of a seer; that is to say, I saw their energy. They are very strong."

"I came down from the waterfall as fast as I could, but they were faster. By the time I got there, they had hypnotized you and taken you away. It was strange, that part...one second you were there, the next I perceived you receding, somehow." He sighed. "That part is hard to explain. But they took your body away. That much is clear to me."

Finally, Johnny found his voice. "So...so, I'm not crazy, then. I really have been dreaming this whole time." He barked a short laugh.

Milos nodded. "Since that day at the waterfall. You're dreaming, but in the waking world. Your dreaming body has solidity and corporeality, probably due to how strongly you've believed in its reality, but you might find that will change in the near future." His face was thoughtful.

"But how am I doing it? And why don't I wake up?"

Milos glanced at the faces of his friends, then back to Johnny. "We're not sure...but I have an idea about it. I think your captors are facilitating this state – perhaps with some sort of drug, or maybe by direct energetic manipulation. As I said, they are quite powerful."

Johnny sat very still, concentrating on his breath, which seemed real enough. He noticed suddenly that there was more light in the air, though the fire had died to nothing more than dully glowing embers. The import of Milos' words was not lost on him, but he felt that whatever mind he had left was full to the point of bursting. Again, his eyes wanted to close. He felt like he was floating on the air, moving with the bite of the night breeze.

"None of that, now," Milos said sharply. "Attention is a choice. You must stand up, shake it off. You are the peerless dreamer! You don't need rest. All you need is to reposition yourself. Come on, now, Johnny...come on..."

But the words faded, the seer's voice lost in a rush of sound like wind through a cavern. More voices swirled – *"You're losing him!"* – but were lost in the persistent sound of that wind. For a time that was outside time, the swirling, ripping wind tore his mind from him, and he existed only in an unfelt, bodiless gray void.

Chapter 5

LAB ONE was a zoo these days, and it was giving Simon DaLuge a headache. Techs in green scrubs milled this way and that, seemingly at random, though he knew this appearance to be deceiving. Groups of white-frocked scientists, each DaLuge's minion in his or her own right, clustered at tables throughout the room, each working on some aspect of the motherboard project.

None of this concerned him.

Oh, there was always a possibility that something could go wrong at one of these menial stations, but DaLuge had overseen this project from the outset, had hand-picked his people for a combination of brilliance and a lack of personal motivation, and he was pretty certain that the computer itself was not a problem.

But the voice in the back of his mind – the one that insisted there was a huge defect in the imaging generators – would not go away. It ate at him night and day, a worm in his consciousness whose effect was now being felt as a lack of sleep and monstrous irritability with those around him.

Thank God for Sneed.

The little man had been nothing short of a blessing. He had moved upward in DaLuge's estimation with astounding speed, filling every gap with his no-nonsense approach and impeccable punctuality. He'd taken over as DaLuge's right-hand man, running interference with the heads of the various lesser departments, diplomatically handling each and every crisis so his boss could focus on what was really important – finishing the motherboard and preparing to install the most sophisticated computer system ever invented.

The Supercontroller.

Simon felt almost sorry for Daniel. The clone was anything but average, and with the combination of hyper-developed brainwave activity and the normal glandular changes of an adolescent, his day-to-day experience must be excruciating.

DaLuge sighed, snapped from his reverie by the voice of one of the young female techs...a Joanie, or maybe it was Janie. "Yes?"

"Sorry to bother you, sir," she said. "You have a call. Sneed said it was important."

"Thank you." He slid his glasses up on his forehead and rubbed his eyes, trying to focus. He knew who it was, and it wasn't a call he was looking forward to.

He stumbled blearily to his main work station and slid into his chair with a weary sigh, rubbing at his eyes again. He let his spectacles slide back down onto his nose, then keyed up the call screen.

"Christ, Simon, you look terrible." Lazaro Sol's voice rumbled through the room. "You're making me feel better about myself."

DaLuge's laugh was gritty and tired. "I'm fine, sir," he said.

Lazaro narrowed his eyes and pursed his lips. "Still worried about your little problem?"

"Well..." DaLuge hesitated, about to go on, but Lazaro cut him off. "Forget about it for a minute," he said, waving a desultory hand in the air. "I've got something else for you."

"Oh?"

"Yes, I'm sending you a recording of a video feed from the raid yesterday. It's only a partial recording, because everything happened so fast. Even Kirkland seems a little stunned by the whole thing, although his military training seems to be holding and he's keeping his questions to himself. Thank the gods that Daniel was busy and didn't witness this event. I'm not sure how I could explain it to him – I can't even explain it to myself just yet."

DaLuge's interest was piqued. He glanced at the small time-bar on the side of the screen, saw that the feed had finished downloading. "Would you like me to look at it now, sir? While I've got you here?"

Lazaro Sol waved a limp hand in the air again. "No, no – take your time and study it, see what you can come up with. Call me back in an hour or two."

He screwed up his eyes, peering through the screen with his black, tarry gaze. "If we're dealing with a superweapon, we need to know right away. Lord knows how such technology was developed, but I think it was excellent foresight on your part to request that their head scientist be kept alive. That was a solid move, and if he proves useful, I won't forget it."

"All right, sir." DaLuge's head was spinning as the screen went blank.

A superweapon? What in all hells could he be talking about?

He opened the video feed and began to watch, grateful for the distraction.

✳✳✳✳✳

Unfortunately, the quality of the feed was low – a chopper returning from the lower part of the valley had caught what appeared to be the tail end of some sort of fight. But it was a fight unlike any that DaLuge had ever seen; indeed, he was having trouble putting the whole thing in context.

He'd slowed it down, tried to clean up the resolution to the best of his abilities, but the image was simply not clear enough. He'd thought of using digital re-creation enhancement software, but what the screen showed was clearly something he'd never seen before, and he thought the software probably wouldn't be able to deal with it either.

Finally, he'd simply sat back and watched it, over and over for half an hour or more.

The chopper's camera had only picked up the last forty-five seconds or so of the skirmish – if one could call it a skirmish when one man lays waste to forty or so.

If one could call it a man.

That was the problem – he simply couldn't tell what he was looking at. The man-like image was a blur on the screen. And slowing down the video replay didn't help at all – whatever the thing was, it had moved at such a speed that it seemed to be simultaneously at one side of the clifftop plain and the other, killing soldiers with savage ferocity.

It was only near the very end, when the soldiers had somehow managed to get a lock on the thing, that the image clearly showed human features. And that was the most disturbing thing about it. If it was human, the blast-guns should have decimated it, rendered it so much twitching meat within only a few rounds.

But – and he had checked this fact against eyewitness accounts that Lazaro

Sol had included with the video clip – the man, or whatever it was, had taken blast after blast simultaneously from some two or three dozen guns, and had not gone down. They had finally blown him (it?) from the edge of the cliff...

"Video pause." The screen came to rest on the image that haunted him. "One hundred fifty percent zoom." The look on the thing's face was definitely, tragically human. Long dark hair blew around an angular face, eyes lit from within, arms caught in mid-pinwheel as it (he?) hung, seemingly in defiance of gravity, its body stretching from the cliff's edge toward the oblivion beyond.

I must be imagining things. Clearly it was a trick of the light.

How the camera had managed to capture this particular string of images at all was beyond him – the chopper's pilot must have had the wherewithal to do it manually. If so, he hoped the pilot's quick thinking would be rewarded with a promotion, or at the least a recommendation.

He sighed and scratched his head. Lazaro Sol had spoken of a superweapon; perhaps his cagey old brain had hit the nail on the head. As unlikely as it was, they had to consider the idea.

******

An hour later DaLuge re-initiated the connection to Lazaro Sol's space-station office. The elderly man's face appeared immediately on the screen. "Well?" he snapped, dismissing all formalities. "What do you think?"

Simon shook his head. "I must say, sir, that I am truly dumbfounded. As you know, that's a hard thing to achieve."

Lazaro pursed his lips and screwed up his face, ancient wrinkles cracking open to reveal new beds of open sores, small as pimples, that were beginning to form. DaLuge shuddered to think what sort of medical hell the old man was going through, and for the first time he realized clearly that Lazaro Sol would not be around much longer – the cancer had simply gotten too much of a hold.

"So," Lazaro said, "It's not just myself, and every other damn person who's seen that feed, then." He narrowed his eyes. "Could this thing be a weapon of some sort?"

"I don't know, sir." Simon pushed his spectacles to the bridge of his nose and blinked twice to clear a sudden rush from his tear-ducts. He felt that he might sneeze, and fought to concentrate. "It...that is to say, the thing, whatever it was, was definitely not operating within human parameters. But if you examine the tape, it definitely has human features." *And human emotions,* he wanted to say, but prudently kept this to himself.

"Hmmm." Lazaro's rheumy eyes glittered like black diamonds. "Human features. Some sort of cyborg? But no...if that were the case, how could it move so fast? Doesn't make sense."

"No, sir, you're right about that," Simon replied. "But according to the report, it killed more than three dozen of your most skilled combat troops, all armed with blast rifles and grenades. Some of them were torn to bits; others looked like their chests had exploded from the inside out. Two of them had their heads torn clean from their necks."

Lazaro Sol kept quiet. He'd seen it all for himself, of course, and knew that Simon was just talking it out, trying to come up with an idea. It was a process he was quite familiar with himself.

"So," DaLuge continued, "it's capable of killing, no doubt. But is it some sort of aberration – some humanoid mutant, perhaps? Something...I don't know...alien, maybe? Or holographic technology – it's theoretically possible, but highly improbable. But then, that's the problem here. I can't come up with a scenario that isn't extremely low on the probability scale. I can theorize, but that's about it."

"Yes. Yes, you're right, Simon. But I think we have an ace in the hole here."

DaLuge thought he knew what the old man was getting at. "The scientist. The one we brought in. You think he might know something?"

"I do. According to your own analysis, their security systems were very sophisticated, and he's the one we pegged as having the most information about them."

"You want me to go talk to him?" DaLuge had to admit that the idea had crossed his own mind. Since studying the technology of the forest encampment, he had begun to develop a certain respect for the man.

"I think it might be an interesting conversation," Lazaro said. "Take Daniel with you, if you want. I'm sure any information he assimilates from this man Stark would be welcome, as he's trying to win over the loins of a certain young lady from the man's own home. And it will serve as one more distraction."

"So, he hasn't taken her yet?" DaLuge was amused.

Lazaro laughed, a cracked, demented sound. "Oh, I think he's waiting for permission from this one," he said, then stifled a cough. "Again, this suits our purposes. It's tragically romantic, if you think about it. And a little comic."

"Well, I'll go talk to the scientist tomorrow," DaLuge said. "I have to finishing aligning the REMenergy generators tonight. We can't power this motherhumping mainframe with standard electricity, as I'm sure you remember."

Lazaro Sol laughed again. The sound made Simon nauseous. "Oh, I haven't forgotten. Another bit of irony. Harnessing the dreams of the world's people to power a system that will eventually rule them – only you could have imagined something so wonderful, Simon. And so diabolical."

"Thank you, sir. I..." But Lazaro Sol had dropped the connection with his usual abruptness. The screen went blank.

DaLuge sat for a moment, relishing the quiet of his small cubby, then typed a note into his personal log to remind him to visit the captive scientist tomorrow. This done, he stood and stretched his back, wincing at the popping sounds it made, then made his way out to the main floor again.

So much hanging in the balance – so much yet to do. And only eleven days to do it.

He dry-swallowed two caffeine pills and went back to work.

CHAPTER 6

THE DESERT SUN *is bright across the cracked plain, and he awakens to the glare, blinking slowly.*

In the distance, sawtooth mountains rise into a pristine razor-blue sky of impossible depth. A couple of coyotes circle through a patch of green prickly cacti beyond the leaning, haphazard slat fence that rings the bare yard, and a scorpion scuttles out from under the steps, clacks its pincers twice and makes off into the shade of the porch.

"Good morning." The voice startles him, not because it is unexpected but because it is male...and somehow familiar. He blinks twice, rubs sleep out of his eyes and stands up unsteadily, refusing to remain confined to his chair this time. He beholds the speaker, a tall man who sits in the old woman's rocker, his tall, thin frame poking out of it at odd angles. "Do you remember who I am?" The man asks.

The face is familiar, and Johnny strains to remember. The name doesn't come at first, but there is recognition there, regardless. "I'm...dreaming." The words are awkward. "Is that right?" He looks down, pinches flesh between two fingers. The pain is exactly what it should be. "It doesn't feel like it."

"This is no dream, any more than that other world where you met me last...well, last night, according to what passes for time over there. But no matter – what I mean is, this world is as real as that one. It is you who are the dreamer, both here and there, but your dreaming body more closely resembles the real thing in this place."

"Martuk. That's your name." The memory fills itself in all at once, and he sees their faces, and remembers himself, and Compound West, and Maia.

"Good. So you do remember."

Johnny rubs his arms, shivers and looks around. "Where's the old lady that's always here?"

As he's finishing his sentence, the door at the end of the porch opens and she hobbles out, holding a tray with a large glass pitcher, three stoneware cups and a plate of sugar cookies on it. "Here, one of you get the door, would you?" She asks.

In a flash, Martuk is out of his chair and pulling the creaking door shut behind her...but before it closes, Johnny sees a strange, subterranean blue glow coming from behind it, and a cold wind blows out, full of an earthy, familiar smell, like medicine and fungus and rot, all rolled together into one.

She sets down the tray and sinks into her rocker with a grateful sigh. Martuk stretches his long frame and lolls against one of the porch's support posts.

"So...what am I doing here?" Johnny asks. He takes a cookie from the plate and bites into it; it's warm, straight from the oven. He takes a cup and washes it down with cold, strong tea while he waits, but neither of them answers at first. Instead, he senses them sharing a covert glance. The old woman pats the pockets of her apron, pulls out her pipe and tobacco, loads and tamps and finally lights it without saying a word. When the tobacco is going strong, she puffs out smoke and looks balefully at the tall man leaning on the rail of the porch. "You tell 'im," she says. "I'm tired of repeating myself."

Martuk grins.

"What?" Johnny asks, almost belligerent.

Even smiling, the tall man seems almost sad. "I'm only a guest here," he says with a sigh, raising his shoulders in a shrug. "But this is your home – don't you remember? This is where you live. J'ualla made this place for you, long ago...or so she tells me."

Johnny squints at the old woman, then back at Martuk, confused. "Who?"

Martuk sighs and sits on the rail. He removes his hat and scratches his head with an over-exaggerated, almost comical gesture. "I guess you're right," he says to the old woman. "He only remembers half of himself here, and the other half over there. Until the two sides can see each other, nothing can change and he'll be bound to infinite repetition. What a shame!"

She only laughs, good-humored. "It's all right. I'm persistent, and there's more than enough time. I feel sorry for you and your companions, though. He won't remember any of this, once I send him back." She cackles. "He'll know who you are, of course, but he won't remember me, or this house, or this conversation."

Martuk shakes his head with a rueful grin. "I'll do what I can," he says, "but..."

She interrupts with a laugh and the wave of a hand. "You disappoint me, Martuk," she says. "There's nothing you can do, or have you forgotten? That timeline was completed long ago – it's over and done. At any rate, you won't be going back for a while, either way. Now that you've so cleverly found my little world, I've got a few things for you to do before you return."

"Oh?" He looks surprised, and more than a bit curious. "Such as...?"

She grins and knocks out her pipe against the rail. "Oh, this and that," she says. "In the meantime, my forgetful young friend here has another leg of his journey to re-live – maybe then he will finally remember." She waves, and the scene begins to recede, moving away into the ether at the speed of dreams.

A hollow rushing replaces all sound, and the lost becomes, once again, found.

CHAPTER 7

SIMON DALUGE hurried down the softly lit white hallway, unmindful of the green-frocked nurses and white-coated lab techs whose elbows he jostled and whose wide-eyed stares followed him as he rushed back to his personal office. In the right-hand pocket of his white lab overcoat, his fingers clutched the reason for his excitement.

He took a shortcut he knew through a stock-room and emerged in a non-secure area of the complex, his fast walk now nearly a run. He flew by a gaggle of visiting students, clustered around one of Clifftop's resident tour-guides, wondering for a moment what they must think of him as he hustled by, coat flapping out behind him like the tattered colors of some buccaneer galleon. He hadn't shaved in days, and he couldn't remember the last time he'd run a comb through his mop of hair. Somehow the image was comical, and he chuckled to himself, grateful for a humorous thought to ground him. These last few months had been intense to say the least, and now, finally! A ray of hope – a light at the end of the tunnel.

Maybe.

He finally slowed to a walk as he approached the lift-chute that would take him into the bowels of the place, the secure area that housed Clifftop's most interesting projects, including most of those he was in charge of. It wouldn't do to have any of his underlings or various minions seeing him in such a state. He had a ship to run, after all. He smoothed back his hair and entered the lift in as dignified a state as he could muster, heart beating in anticipation. He nodded to the other man sharing the lift with him, whom he recognized as one of Lazaro Sol's cronies.

Ashbro. That's his name.

He had a moment of curiosity over the man's presence here. Certainly, as a full Elder, he had the clearance for it, but most of the Elders who came here stayed away from the innermost workings of the place. They preferred to leave the scientists to their jobs, whiling away their time instead at some of the various leisure pursuits afforded by the luxury of Clifftop. They mostly treated this place as a vacation spot, and he couldn't blame them. In many ways, this was a finer place of accommodation than many hotels DaLuge had visited in the course of his long career.

It was only a few moments' ride to Lab One, and then another few to walk to the solitude of his private office, which doubled as his own personal scaled-down laboratory. His fingers shook as he took the sample slide from his pocket, and he nearly dropped it twice.

The scanner's tensile mechanism locked the slide into place and the transparent lid snapped shut with a smooth click. The machine began to do its thing, humming quietly to itself like a contented librarian.

DaLuge went to an alcove in the corner of the room and rooted through a stainless steel cupboard until he found what he was looking for – a small, old-fashioned coffee pot. He turned it on and went through the old, comfortable ritual. He hadn't had a cup in almost five years, but he thought he could use one today. The beans he had were pre-ground and freeze-dried, but still not terrible after years of storage. He poured in the water, and the contraption began to perk and bubble. Within a few moments, the smell of fresh coffee began to drift to his nostrils, and a small smile crept across his face.

Gods! I feel better than I have in years!

It might be a mistake to become overconfident, but he knew he was onto something.

He reached back into the cupboard and pulled out one more thing – a small, flat tin. He opened it and his smile widened. There were still half a dozen imported Turkish cigarettes there, old and probably a bit stale, but good nonetheless. He breathed deeply, and the smell of the tobacco combined with the coffee's odor to produce a heady feeling, a pang he hadn't felt in a long time.

He'd given up tobacco around the same time as coffee, but he had a feeling that it might be a good time to re-introduce himself to a couple of old friends. He poured a fresh cup, took a cigarette from the tin, and slid into the chair in front of his personal workspace-slash-desk. He lit the cigarette with a hand-held torch he used for soldering small components in his workshop, drew deeply, and exhaled a fragrant cloud, his smile widening. He closed his eyes, sipped contentedly at the fresh hot brew, and waited for the scanner to finish, letting the events of the day wash over him.

*****

Sneed had alerted him this morning.

"Preliminary scans show that the mutated tissue on the girl's face has some very interesting qualities."

"What kind of qualities?" DaLuge was distracted, trying his best not to snap at the younger man. Sleepless nights and stress were taking their toll.

"Well, according to testing on a routine sample taken the day before yesterday, the swollen discolorations on her face and neck are the result of the sequencers' first attempt to establish neural contact." He extended a sheaf of papers to Simon. "I've got the reports right here. I know you're busy, but I thought it might be important to you."

"Yes, yes, let me see." He grabbed the papers with a little more snap and gusto than he'd meant to, thought of apologizing for it, then decided against it. Gods! This job was getting to him.

Sneed stood with his hands locked behind his back, unaffected, waiting for his boss. DaLuge let his eyes run the course of the first page, slowed a bit by the second. By the time he'd reached the top of page three, his mind was alight with a genuinely new and fascinating idea – one that could potentially solve the problem of the imaging generators.

He looked up, letting his face relax into the first real smile he'd had for a very long time. "Mr. Sneed," he said, clapping the man on the shoulder. "You have done a fine thing here. Thank you for bringing this to my attention. You might have just saved my goddamned life."

*****

The beep of the scanner brought him back to the moment. He took a last drag from the cigarette, crushed it out and washed it down with the last of his coffee. Pushing these distractions impatiently aside, he sent the test results to the personal screen on his desk and pulled up a chair to begin the real work.

Within ten minutes, he pushed away from the desk, eyes alight. He'd seen enough, and it would work! By the gods, it would work. He gave a silent prayer of thanks to whatever deity had kept the girl alive this whole time and punched the desk-com unit.

"Sneed!" he growled, not waiting for a reply before continuing. "Go to the main terminal and run a search for a folder named 'imaging generators', then another one called 'supercontroller suit', then...hell, scratch that, just dump the entire contents of the hard drive onto a card and get someone to run it down here. I have some shit to do!!" He laughed at his own elation. It had been awhile since his intuition had really paid off, and it felt good to be right. This discovery could change the entire face of the project.

A moment of silence from the com-unit, then: "You okay, boss? You sound a little excited."

"You're damn right I'm excited. Don't worry about me, just do what I asked."

"All right, sir. Give me twenty minutes."

"Good boy, Sneed. DaLuge out." He immediately keyed the unit's 'send' button again. "Sneed? One more thing. Actually, two things. Get me some decent cigarettes and some good ground coffee beans. I feel an all-nighter coming on."

CHAPTER 8

THE MORNING SUN was bright on the rolling green hills as Johnny blinked into full awareness. The first thing he noticed was how good he felt. His body felt whole, real, and energized. He took a deep breath and looked around slowly, trying to orient himself.

Milos was there, exactly where Johnny had last seen him, squatting over the remains of the last night's fire, poking at the embers with a long sharp stick. Esmerelda was curled, sleeping peacefully on a blanket with her back to the mossy side of the log she'd shared with Johnny during the previous evening's palaver. Oddly, she looked quite comfortable.

The stump where Janet had sat through the night's stories was unoccupied, but Johnny heard snapping sounds from the brush behind him and thought it likely that the stout woman was the one making them. There was no sign of Martuk, and his tent was gone; or rather, the ragged piece of canvas that had been the tent lay flat, folded over into a neat pile. Atop the canvas were four tent-pegs and two lengths of twine, now neatly coiled. The ground had been swept clean and then littered with a random assortment of pine needles, dead twigs and a scattering of fresh dirt, so that there was very little to tell of their night's stay.

Janet hove into view, carrying a few dead sticks and dry fodder, which she unceremoniously dumped beside Milos. He fed the sticks into the heat of the leftover embers, then took off his hat and began to wave it steadily above the coals. Within a minute, a small, perky fire was crackling. Near Johnny's feet, Esmerelda began to stir.

Milos stood up, catching Johnny's eye as he did.

"Well, well," he said with a broad grin, putting his hands on the small of his back. "If it isn't the peerless dreamer. I thought you might be back this morning." He twisted, first one way and then the other, and his back made a series of popping sounds. "Did you have a nice trip?"

"Where did I go?" Johnny was confused. "Last I knew, I was sitting right here on this log, but then..." He frowned. "I don't know. I seem to remember something..."

Suddenly, with no premeditation, he jumped to his feet with a fluid movement and did a backward triple somersault along the length of the log, only aware after the moment had passed that he'd done anything at all. He looked at Milos sheepishly.

"What the hell was that?" he asked, bewildered.

Janet guffawed, a chugging sound that was genuinely funny in its own right.

Milos laughed. "Well, aren't we feeling fine this morning! To answer your first question, you didn't go anywhere, because you're not really here to begin with. Oh, but you already know that. And yet, here you are anyway." He shrugged. "So there you are."

He laughed and looked off into the distance, feigning interest in something that wasn't there, then back at Johnny. "Are you ready to travel, Monsignor Perdue?" He gave the words a little trill, but merry as he seemed, his eyes were cold and direct. "Methinks the time has come for the intrepid travelers to embark upon their epic journey, at which conclusion they shall rescue the princess, or break their bodies upon the battlements of yon castle."

Esmerelda sighed loudly and sat up straight. "Oh, give the kid a break," she said crossly, seeing Johnny's look of general confusion. "He means we're going to go after Maia. Good morning, by the way." She smiled, her face lighting. "It's nice to see you again. We thought we'd lost you."

"But where did I go?" he repeated.

"We should talk about these things on the trail," Milos said. "And I need some breakfast. This could be a long day. In the meantime, you shouldn't try to understand it all. Just enjoy the morning. We'll be moving soon enough."

He began to methodically lay out an array of flat wooden bowls. On each, he placed a hunk of the bread that was left over from the previous evening.

From somewhere nearby, he produced a beat-up old metal skillet, a small sack with a few potatoes in it, and a lumpy, greasy parcel that turned out to be raw meat. He set the potatoes aside and pulled the strips of meat apart, laying them neatly in the pan.

"Venison," he said, noticing Johnny watching him. "This is the last of the uncooked stuff. The rest is smoked and jerked. I'd offer you some, but I suppose you're still not hungry." He laid the pan across a corner of the fire. Within moments, the meat began to sizzle, releasing a tantalizing odor into the morning air.

Johnny laughed, a little uneasily. "I feel great," he said, but he realized that what Milos said was true – though the smell of the cooking meat was fine, it was only a part of an entire, composite sensory experience. There were no hunger pangs; indeed, the experience of the odor seemed unconnected to his body in any way.

He looked around. Janet had picked up the canvas, tent-pegs and twine and tightly packed the whole thing together into a compact roll. She looped a short piece of twine around it and cinched it tight, then tied it to her pack.

"So," Johnny said, "where's Martuk? Or did I just imagine him?"

"Oh, he's around," Milos replied. "He packed up and left when you did. I think he followed you. He's trying very hard to help you, you know."

"I appreciate that," Johnny said slowly, "but I'm having a difficult time wrapping my mind around it all. Especially when I wake up here, it's morning, and I feel....well, like I said, I feel great! My body feels fantastic. But I guess it's not real, right?"

Esmerelda was up and moving now, busily packing odds and ends unneeded for finishing with breakfast.

"Describe how you feel," Milos said. He picked up a small piece of bread, popped it in his mouth and chewed methodically, watching Johnny's reaction.

Johnny took the question seriously and thought for a moment before responding. "I feel normal," he said at last. "Or at least how I think normal should feel. I think I've felt this way before, but I don't remember how long ago that was. And since the waterfall with Maia, I haven't felt even close to normal." He shuddered. "It's been a nightmare, if you want to know the truth."

At this, Milos and Janet broke up in gales of laughter. Johnny wanted to be insulted, but the feeling was impossible to summon. Instead he grinned. "Ha ha," he said. "I guess that was a little funny."

"I'm sure it's been very difficult," Esmerelda said. Her voice was at once melodious and soothing. "We're here to help, though; strange as we may seem to you, I think Milos is right when he says that fate and power have brought you to us. And you may yet be able to help us, as well."

Johnny laughed again. It felt good to laugh. It was nice to know that, corporeal or not, one could still find the humor in things. "How could I help you?" he asked. "If what you're telling me is the truth, I'm not much more than a ghost, anyway."

"Ah, but nothing could be further from the truth!" Milos' tone was sharp, but his eyes were kind. "I've seen what you can do for myself. And with our help, you can do infinitely more!"

"I don't understand." Johnny frowned. "I haven't done anything! At least not that I know of."

Milos looked closely at Johnny, seeming to study him with a sweep of his eyes. It was a look Johnny had seen before, and it unnerved him. "Do you remember what happened on the upper plain, just the other day? The day Maia was taken." Milos' tone was casual, but his gaze burned with knowledge.

Johnny's eyes widened, and he gasped, taken by a sudden inward convulsion of thought...but Milos continued speaking as if he had no idea of the potent, violent memories his simple question had triggered. "The thing you must realize is that everything at its most basic level is the same kind of energy," he said. "This energy permeates everything. It is our source, our power, and its very essence is one of vital, dynamic change. Dreaming energy is no different; in fact, when properly harnessed, it's an incredibly potent type of energy. Human beings normally don't utilize it – mostly because they don't know it exists, or that it can have any practical use. And yet somehow you have rallied your dreaming energy into the form we see now." He held Johnny with his stare, eyes challenging. "Let me tell you something, Johnny. You are something that none of ever expected to see; a pure-energy doppelgänger with seemingly no limits to his energetic capability. You are the peerless dreamer, young Perdue! Do you know what that means?"

But Johnny was lost, turning inward, his memories muttering like a room full of sullen, sleeping children. "I killed them," he said suddenly. His eyes went dark; breath had stopped, unnoticed, in his chest. Memory surfaced, ponderous and weighty. "All those soldiers," he whispered. He looked up at Milos, filled with awe. "On the plain. The day Maia was taken. I killed a lot of soldiers."

His fists clenched at the memory, and a ripple of power spiked through him, a killing heat that flowed from every point of his body at once, exploding like a solar flare. For a moment, the fire roared bright, and a shower of sparks exploded upward into the morning air.

Milos jumped backward quickly, only just avoiding an ember that fell and floated, tumbling earthward. His eyes gleamed. "Ahhhh!" he husked. "So you do remember! Good! Good!" He nodded appreciatively. "We'll work on your memories more at a later time."

He flipped the meat expertly from the pan, piling a more or less equal share on each plate to go with the bread he'd already doled out. "In the meantime – breakfast is served. Get it while it's hot – I'll start cooking these potatoes."

*****

Breakfast was over quickly, and again Johnny was amazed at the pure efficiency of the group. Nothing was said about it, and he couldn't pick out any particular pattern as far as who had what job, but the camp was cleaned, the fire scattered, and packs slung over shoulders before he'd had even a moment to consider what was happening.

But then, how long is a moment when you are a dream? It seemed that time itself was no longer a constant. The more he thought about what he'd learned during the previous evening's education, the weirder it all seemed – but still there was no fear.

It seemed that he should be afraid, indeed by any normal standard he should have been completely out of his mind...but he wasn't. If Milos and his peculiar companions were to be believed, his body was less than solid, but it seemed solid enough. His movements felt normal; in fact, better than normal. His body was all there, minus normal bodily urges, but stronger and more lithe than it had ever been. He felt constantly on the verge of laughter, but settled for a smile, enjoying the brisk morning breeze and the fresh dewy scent of grass and pine.

"Ready, Johnny?" Milos asked as he hoisted a pack across his broad shoulders.

Esmerelda was already a hundred yards ahead, moving westward like a wraith through the tall, waving meadow grass towards a distant line of trees that murked into the blue hills beyond. She was followed by Janet, and then

Milos, who walked away without a backward glance. Johnny brought up the rear, unanswered questions boiling in his mind.

*****

The only sounds were their feet on the trail and the occasional whisper of cloth as it scraped against grass or a tree branch. Johnny's boots kicked up dust and left tracks in the dirt, and he began, for the first time since this strange condition had begun, to gauge himself, to notice what he could and couldn't do. Trying not to draw attention to himself, he stopped for a moment, squatted, and slapped his hand against the waving grass beside the trail.

The grass moved as it should, as it encountered the space that was supposed to be his hand. He felt the pressure of it, the way the blades swished across his skin, but something was missing...something vital. He stood, clenching and unclenching his hands, trying to figure out what it was. After a moment, he gave up and began moving again. The women had gotten quite a ways ahead now, and he began to move faster to catch up.

Milos had stopped beside the trail and apprehended him as he approached. "Figuring it all out?" he asked, as if aware of what Johnny was thinking.

"Maybe."

Milos seemed to scan him with those piercing eyes. "These creatures – the ones that took your body...have you had contact with them?" His voice was gentle as the breeze. Johnny felt his consciousness drift, and knew that the sorcerer was affecting him.

"Are you trying to hypnotize me?" His voice came from a long way off, swishing through the grass like a zephyr. Images swam in his eyes, as if through liquid glass.

With a rush, he came back to the moment to find Milos peering at him, doing that peculiar thing he did which made Johnny feel that his very soul was open, bared to the the cold wind of scrutiny. The seer looked away with a smile. "Good, good," he said, and mimed patting Johnny on the back.

They both laughed, and after a moment, Milos began to walk again, following the faint trail through the grass. "We'll dig a little deeper later on, probably with Martuk's help," he said. "I believe that with only a little effort, we should be able to help you reconstruct the totality of your memories since the time of your abduction. Then we should have a much better idea of what's happened to you. And I must admit, I am very interested to find out more about these creatures."

"Oh." Johnny felt a sudden wave of very real fear, and experienced a moment of vertigo. Milos must have sensed what he was feeling, because he stopped immediately and turned to face him.

"Don't worry." His eyes conveyed empathy and humor. "Just remember, you're not even here to begin with. The part of you that can die is far away, and by all accounts it seems that your body is growing stronger, rather than the other way around. How could you have anything to fear? Use your energy!" He reached out suddenly with his right hand, seemed to reach *inside* Johnny.

Time slowed to a crawl. White light arced from Milos' hand, and suddenly Johnny was surrounded by a skein of living energy, a field of uncharted immensity that surrounded and permeated himself and everything else. It was the essence of everything. Within some previously unplumbed depth of himself, he knew beyond the shadow of a doubt that he was seeing the world with sorcerer's eyes.

Within the field were all things, both real and imagined, and he saw himself and Milos as points of awareness, floating in a sea of pure energy. The energy flowed in ropes and lines from every point simultaneously. The objects of the world – grass, trees, sky – were rendered pale and transparent, thin as a reflection...and he knew that was just what they were.

Nothing is 'real'. All things are energy. Consciousness and awareness are the connecting strings of the universe.

After an eternity which might have been a second or an hour, his vision returned to normal, and he was left with a feeling of the purest bliss he'd ever encountered. His entire being seemed to be turned inside out, tilted upward in an ecstatic smile that reached to the heavens. Above them, the sky stirred with shades and subtle hues of greens and pinks that he'd never noticed before, though he knew now that they had been there the whole time.

"Perception is like a window," the sorcerer's voice came on a sighing wind. "It must be cleaned if you are to witness the wonders of the world. Let go of all you know of your human self. Your body is unreachable – so be it! Accept what you are now, learn to utilize your dreaming energy, and you can go to unimaginable places and learn unbelievable things. Dreaming is the key, and you are already there. Your good fortune is astounding! Learn to move, to flow out along the lines of perception, and all universes are yours to explore."

How do I do that?

The thought was an instantaneous spark, and Milos' smile broadened. "Aha!" he said. "You're getting there! You just sent me that thought without trying to speak out loud. A very good, economical use of your energy. This is something I've taught many an apprentice, but always while dreaming together. Normally it's very difficult to do in a waking state, but that's the beauty of what you are. You're bridging a gap that has never been bridged! You were able to send that thought just now as if it was nothing. This is the beginning of what I'm trying to teach you. You moved a thought along the lines of perception. Next time you should try moving your whole being – a true leap of awareness."

Why are you helping me?

Milos shrugged. "A few reasons. Partially a normal sense of helpfulness, but that's not it – not really. If I'm being honest, it's mostly because I'm extremely curious about how you are able to do what you're doing, and I want to learn more about your strange captors. And I'm sure you would like to see Maia freed, which is a goal we have quite in common."

Johnny said nothing, and after a moment Milos began to walk along the trail again, humming to himself.

Johnny followed. He didn't know if he was walking or merely floating along, but it didn't seem to matter. Above them, the spring sunshine pushed away towering clouds and the immediate threat of rain. In the nearby trees, the *caawww* of a crow was the only, lonely sound.

*****

From the topmost branch of a lightning-split snag at the edge of the forest, a huge raven with shimmering white feathers watched the progress of the travelers from glittering, platinum eyes. When they were gone, it spread its wings into the rising breeze, wheeled and disappeared along the lines of perception.

Chapter 9

John Stark sat on the floor of his room, wrapped in the one small blanket he'd been given, hugging his knees to his chest in an attempt to keep warm. He'd long ago given up trying to finagle another blanket from the guards that brought his meals twice a day – they were stony-faced and unresponsive to his questions and protests.

There was an attitude of surly menace about them that bothered him. Something – or rather a lack of something – in their eyes. He had no doubt that if he were to attempt an escape and be captured by one of them, he'd be swatted like a fly. It was not a prospect he enjoyed thinking about.

He coughed twice, hawked and spat into the small trash receptacle by the foot of the bed. The cough bothered him – it was dry and hurt a little. But it was nothing to the rage he felt at being trapped, contained like this with no knowledge of the fate of his people, or of what was to happen to him.

He'd been keeping track of the days as well as possible by counting the number of meager meals he received, and the changes of the guard, which he heard as muffled footfalls through the door, four times a day.

So he was surprised when, on the fourth day after his capture, he heard footsteps approaching his cell only an hour or so after the last guard change. From the sound of it, there were at least two people outside his door, maybe three.

He stood up, wincing at the pins and needles in his feet, and stepped forward to greet them...whoever they were. If they were here for his life, then he would go to meet his fate with what dignity remained in him.

The door opened with a clang of releasing locks, and three men stepped inside. A fourth waited just outside the door, and this one Stark noted immediately, sizing him up for later review. He was a small, thin man with a sallow complexion and pallid skin. He wore a gray felt hat, and the look he gave Stark was cold and empty. There was something about him that reminded John of the look of the clone guards...but one could easily see that this man was infinitely more clever.

The others were of a different sort. Stark wouldn't have said that he liked them, exactly, but there was nothing immediately threatening about them. The one obviously in charge was a tall, bony man with a shock of gray-white frizz and half-spectacles which sat atop the bridge of his none-too-small proboscis. He was wearing a long white coat with many pockets, out of which poked a frightening array of pens, small tools and scraps of paper.

Behind him were two younger men. One was short, with a square face and trimmed, dark brown hair. He held a clipboard and seemed to defer to the older, white-haired man, but it was the third person that caught Stark's attention.

For one thing, he was younger than any of the others in the room, as evidenced by the remaining baby fat around his cheeks and his searching, nervous eyes. These were the traits that belied his adolescence, but under that first impression was something else – a shrewd, ancient intelligence that seemed to hang off him like an ill-fitting coat.

Stark would have liked a few moments just to study this fascinating man-child, but before he could, the white-haired man spoke.

"Hello, sir," the man said. "I'm not too happy that we must make our acquaintance under such severe circumstances, but it is a pleasure to meet you, nonetheless. I'm Simon DaLuge, and this is my assistant, Sneed. This..." he indicated the young man who'd captured Stark's attention, "...this is young master Daniel. He's here in a mostly observatory capacity. We'd like to ask you some questions, if that's all right."

Stark answered cautiously, keeping his tone flat and even. "Okay," he said. "Maybe if you ask the right questions, I'll feel like answering 'em."

"Why don't we go down the hall?" DaLuge surveyed the room with a cold eye. "There's an empty conference room that might suit our purposes a little better. In fact, now that I'm looking around, I'm going to see to it that you're moved to better quarters." He sniffed the air. "Kind of musty in here. Sneed, can you see to that?"

"Of course. Right away." Sneed riffled through the sheaf of papers clamped to his clipboard and jotted down a note.

DaLuge turned to Stark. "What's your name, sir?" he asked.

Stark looked at him evenly. "There's no reason why that should be important to you," he said. "Why don't you just ask your questions and I'll see if I feel like answering them."

DaLuge laughed apologetically, held up a hand in deference. "All right, all right, if that's the way you feel," he said. "I was just going to ask if you'd like some coffee. I was thinking about having some, myself."

"Oh." Stark relaxed, ever so slightly. "I guess you can call me John," he said. "And I suppose I could use a cup of joe."

✻✻✻✻✻

Stark gasped audibly when he saw the view through the oversized bay windows at the far end of the conference room. Sunlight glinted from an endless expanse of moving water. Far on the horizon, brigades of clouds shifted through a twisting, changing regimen, shades of silver-white in a blue sky that seemed to stretch out interminably.

DaLuge smiled. "Ah, the sea. A beautiful vista, yes? Let's go sit by the window, since you're enjoying it. I don't get a chance to appreciate the view as much as I'd like, anyhow. Sneed? Can you get us some coffee? Dark roast, preferably. Daniel?"

The man-child had not spoken a word during the short trip from Stark's quarters to the conference room. He stood with hands clasped behind his back, studying a series of paintings on one wall. At DaLuge's voice, he turned.

"Yes?"

"I was asking if you would like some coffee."

"Oh." He hesitated, and for the briefest moment his face seemed troubled, as if he wasn't sure what the question meant. "I suppose so."

Sneed left to get the refreshments, and DaLuge gestured with an open hand. "Please, John. After you."

The two of them made their way to the far end of the room, near the large windows. Daniel followed shortly behind, but the other one, the unidentified man with the gray felt hat, stayed beside the door. His purpose as a security measure was obvious.

John Stark had never seen the ocean. He'd seen photos and video, of course – the compound had had an extensive library. But his breath stopped short in his chest as they approached the alcoved windows. The view was spectacular; gulls wheeled and fluttered in the strong wind that beat at the surrounding vegetation, which was plentiful, lush and green.

The room they were in seemed to be on the second or third floor of a structure or series of structures that loomed at least ten stories high, judging by what he could see stretching away to the left of the large window. They were at one end of the mammoth complex, built as a diminished-U shape around an immaculately landscaped topiary maze. Everywhere, there was evidence of culture and control, but he found it odd that they would build this place so close to the wildness of the ocean.

Strange. This doesn't really feel like a prison.

He was acutely aware of the fact that he'd made a lot of assumptions regarding the things that were happening to him, and swore a silent oath not to make the same mistake in the future.

He became aware of DaLuge standing next to him, arms folded over his chest. He, too, was looking out across the expanse, a dreamy, unguarded look in his eye. "Gorgeous, isn't it?" His voice was low.

Stark assessed the other man coolly, aware that DaLuge might be pretending to be friendly and sympathetic in order to win his trust – something Stark had never given away freely to begin with. He wasn't about to start now. Still, there was something he liked about Simon DaLuge, and the man didn't appear to be acting.

Simon sighed and turned away from the view with a shake of his head. "It's too bad," he said. "I've been here for nearly twenty years, and I probably have time to look at the ocean maybe twice in a year. A waste, if you ask me."

Sneed had apparently made short work of his coffee assignment, and now re-appeared with a small tray. It held a steaming pot, three sturdy mugs, spoons, and a small pitcher of cream. Stark found himself cracking a smile despite his best efforts, and allowed DaLuge to pour him a cup. He added a healthy dollop of cream and sat down at the table, stirring the liquid, savoring the smell. Really good coffee had been a rarity at Compound West despite Abby Carmichle's best attempts to cultivate the plant, and he'd been cold and nursing a cough for three days now. He sipped at his cup and relished the warmth as it spread through his chest, still trying to assess these strange people from the corners of his eyes.

The mood in the room was hardly one of interrogation, and this very fact made Stark nervous. *What do they want?*

It seemed obvious. They wanted him to relax, to trust them.

Daniel had taken a cup of coffee and sat down at one end of the table, and now DaLuge pulled up a chair, banging his cup down carelessly. Coffee slopped over the side and ran onto the hard-plastic tabletop. He wiped at it absently with the corner of a napkin.

"I suppose we should get down to business, John," he said. "I hope you don't mind indulging me a bit. I hate to start off on a bad note, and you seem like a stalwart fellow. My intention is not to bully or intimidate you." He smiled. "I figure everyone can appreciate a good cup of coffee." He slurped from his cup, then sat forward with his hands steepled under his chin. His eyes seemed a little too large through his spectacles.

"The truth, John," he said, "is that we need your help."

Stark took four or five measured breaths, counted them down in his head, seeking to control his response.

"My help?" he ventured after a moment. "And what could I possibly help you with? You seem to be holding all the cards."

DaLuge laughed, a sound both brittle and humorless. Stark didn't care for the sound of that laugh. "You would think so, wouldn't you? But I assure you that nothing is further from the truth. If I didn't believe in the essential validity of what we are doing here, I would be scared shitless of all the unknowns – pardon my crude colloquialisms. As it is, we proceed with utmost caution. Nothing is taken lightly, I assure you."

"And what is it that you do here?" Stark asked, surprised by his own boldness. He saw a look exchanged between Daniel and Sneed, who'd taken a quiet seat by the wall.

Simon smiled. "We make the world livable for the next thousand years," he said.

Stark eyed him coldly. "That's a hard concept for me to accept," he said. "What could be the possible reasoning that would allow you to justify the extermination of my people?"

DaLuge's smile was forced. "It's not my job to justify anything," he said. "If you want my opinion, it was a rather hasty solution. More diplomatic means could have been used. But, as I said, that is not my area and I'm getting away from the point."

"Which is...?" Stark couldn't hold back his sneer. "Oh, right. You already told me – you need my help. Well, let me tell you now, bub – I could live for that whole thousand years you're talking about, and I'll never help you. Not on purpose, anyways."

DaLuge rose from his chair, clasped his hands behind his back. All the humor was gone from his face. "I'm going to pretend you didn't say that," he said. "Sneed? Do you have the vid?"

"Yes, sir." Sneed produced a small cartridge and plugged it into the port on the wallscreen behind him. An image jumped into focus, but it took Stark a few moments to put together what he was seeing. When he did, he gasped, and a single name dropped from his astounded lips: "Perdue!"

Chapter 10

Darkness surrounded Maia. She felt her way through a wall of gray fog, blindly groping, fighting off the panic that threatened to leave her stranded in this place, this purgatory, forever.

I am a child of the universe. I am a being of light.

The litany did not help; instinctively, she knew it was worthless here.

Dim red visions swam before her eyes; grotesque, insectile sounds pervaded her consciousness.

Where am I?

A world coalesced, but not the world of everyday. Everywhere, there was dark movement, slippery shadows that moved in dissonant rhythms, beating on eyedrums and earballs till the cacophony nearly drove her mad.

On the jagged, broken edge of sanity, sharpened to a razor point and stained with the blood of those who'd dared venture there, a voice intruded. Simultaneously, she knew she was dreaming, but the thought provided no relief.

Help me.

"Karla?" Maia's voice in the dream was too loud, jagged and grotesque as the dark, shadowy things that moved and groped everywhere, slipping and sliding with hissing, clicking sounds. "Where are we?"

A figure emerged; a shadowed face, swollen beneath clumps of once-blond hair.

The bads got me, Maia. I thought they were going to get Johnny, but they got me instead. The skeeters brought 'em.

"I know, honey. I know." It was unbearable; a wave of sadness hit her, intense and raw, making her feel ill. *Strange,* she thought disconnectedly. *I didn't know you could feel nauseous in a dream.*

Karla spoke, out loud this time, her voice a watery sigh: "It was all so long ago. I can't remember it all. I think I should be old by now."

The darkness had receded, if only a bit, and the strange shapes that comprised this reality began to take on more familiar forms. It was a room, large and dim.

"What am I seeing, Karla?" The dream was beginning to dissipate, and Maia suddenly wanted nothing more than to hold it together, to stay with Karla as long as she could.

You're seeing my world. The shadows gather forever here.

Even as dream-thought, the girl's voice held an unbearable sadness. Maia felt the sadness as a wave, threatening to overtake her, and she fought to hold the dream just a little longer, pushing back with all the force she could muster.

A strange and terrible light permeated the scene, and now she saw through Karla's eyes again. She'd done this once before, she remembered, and it had been horrible then...more terrible than anything she'd experienced. She'd tried to help the girl, but had shrunk away when she'd realized the truth.

"You're conscious, aren't you?" She whispered, awed and frightened. The room gained more definition – three or four sterile white beds, equipped with hospital machinery, dim white cupboards stocked with the power of life and death. As before, the familiar elements in the room seemed to move in slow motion, and she knew instinctively what she'd known before, but chosen to forget: that Karla was in a hellish eternity, her time-sense stretched beyond forever, a world of pain moving in agonizing slow motion.

The vision spun, and she took a deep breath, knowing she could hold on only a moment longer before she woke up.

"Karla? Are you aware of what's happening to you?"

Make it stop. Please, Maia. Make it stop if you can. The bads...oooh, they're bad.

Maia could contain herself no longer. She screamed, an anguished cry of pain and frustration that seemed to blow her away from contact with Karla's reality. Worlds and visions of worlds flashed by with incredible speed, lights spinning...

✳✳✳✳✳

She was left in the cottony non-world just below waking. She could feel her body, lying on her right side in her room at Clifftop, hands clenched under her soft down pillow. But she was still asleep, still dreaming. The pain from her encounter with Karla was gone, but the memory was vivid.

Milos' voice floated on cloud wings. *You cannot afford to forget any longer. You must put yourself together while you're awake.*

A terrible, lonely feeling swept through her, an incomparable sigh from the secret recesses of her deepest being. *What if I can't?*

The sorcerer's shape emerged from the mist, a dark figure with glowing eyes. *You know the truth. You think this is only a dream? You are powerful, Maia. And I think you have more than just yourself to consider now.*

What do you mean?

Milos' features were clear now, his ruddy face sober and honest. He stood with his arms at his sides, and a scene began to coalesce around him. He spoke aloud. "I think you know." He hesitated, peered at her with his usual smile. "It's good to make contact, Maia. I've been trying to get through to you for a while now."

They were in a meadow in the very early morning. The first cold rays of the sun filtered through a copse of dark spruce, and above them the hills stretched toward the blue-green slopes of mountains.

She gazed around in wonder. "This is real, isn't it?"

He laughed, and the sound was cool as the dew, sparkling on the fresh grass around them. "I wish we could just get around this whole 'real or not real' thing," he said. "But I know what you're saying. You are indeed witnessing a real place; my camp, in fact. Now listen: our time is short. Let's not waste it on trivialities. Soon you will wake up, and it is critical that when you do, you put yourself back together." He said the words with such emphasis that she shivered.

Nearby she could see the camp; a small tent, the smoking remains of a fire. Three or four dim figures lay sleeping around the fire, and one sat hunched over the coals, unmoving, staring with eyes like glowing pits.

"Who is that?" she asked. An uneasy feeling snaked through her belly.

He stared at her, unblinking. The vision had taken on a surreal pall now, and she knew he was right – soon she would wake up back at Clifftop. "That is the peerless dreamer, Maia," he said softly. "You've seen him before. When you put yourself back together, you'll remember him, too." He reached out with his strong, calm hands and grasped her shoulders, turning her face toward his. "Now listen. We're coming for you, Maia, but you have to be strong. You have to be strong, and you have to remember yourself. Put yourself back together, Maia. You can't afford to forget anymore."

"What did you mean when you said that I have more than myself to consider? Everyone else is dead."

That's not what I meant, and you know it.

The vision began to fade, colors melting together. The great vacuum tugged at her, and she felt her body again, lying in bed. An urge of an immediate nature gathered in her stomach, a fluttering there that she'd felt a few times recently, and she awoke with a start, already moving toward the lavatory before she was fully awake.

She almost didn't make it, her gorge rose with such vigor. She vomited into the toilet, twice, three times, then flopped on the floor, spent. Milos' voice kept replaying itself in her mind. And what of the vision of Karla? Had that been real, too?

There was no point in speculation. Her body wracked with another spasm, and she only just got her head above the toilet before she again emptied the contents of her stomach into the receptacle.

You have more than just yourself to think of now, Maia.

Her body knew what he had meant – had, in fact, known for some time. She'd simply been too busy, too saddened, too outraged to notice. Her stomach fluttered and she retched, but without result this time. The toilet flushed itself automatically and small jets on the sides of the bowl sprayed antiseptic, clean-smelling liquids that erased the evidence of her morning sickness. She sank back, leaned against the bathroom wall, feeling the cold hardness of the tile through her thin shirt. Behind her closed lids she could still see his earnest face, eyes burning across the distance.

We're coming for you, Maia.

She thought of the hunched figure she'd seen looking into the deadlight of the coals. The peerless dreamer, Milos had said. *Who was he?* She had a feeling she knew.

You think this is a mere dream?

No...it had been real. What she'd seen was happening, somewhere to the east. Milos and his party drew closer.

I am a child of the universe. I am a being of light.

With a sigh of elation, she leaned her head back against the wall, letting the memories begin to shift, to re-align in her consciousness.

Her hand stole across her stomach, rested there protectively.

Chapter 11

Before they reached the prisoner's quarters that morning, DaLuge had briefed Daniel on what he might expect during the interrogation, but he hadn't paid much attention. His thoughts had been with Maia. He hadn't seen her in a few days, and he wanted to pay her a visit after they were done with this business...whatever it was.

DaLuge was there to interview the old scientist – something about a fight that had apparently broken out on the morning after Daniel had led the invasion of the compound. Daniel seemed to remember some sort of skirmish that morning where a few soldiers had been killed, but they were Kirkland's men, not his. And besides that, he'd been overcome with thoughts of Maia that day...and ever since, for that matter.

When Sneed put the vid-disc in the wallscreen reader, Daniel's curiosity was piqued. But he was nowhere near ready for the image that popped on the screen. Luckily, his reaction was masked by that of the captured scientist, John Stark.

"Perdue!"

The man was startled, no doubt about it. Fighting down his own initial reaction, Daniel studied the image on the screen, a close-up still of a face that he recognized...the face that inspired that odd feeling that he found so disquieting.

Jealousy.

It was the young man, or someone who looked a lot like him – the one he'd seen making love to Maia that day in the forest, when he had first discovered the compound. He felt his face grow hot at the memory, and a feeling washed through his stomach that was equal parts anger and shame.

But his reaction was not nearly as violent as that of the old man who now stared at the screen, mouth open, eyes glazed. Stark licked his lips a few times, looking from one to the other of them.

"You know what you're looking at?" DaLuge studied him with narrowed eyes. Daniel had seen that look before, in Grandfather's eyes. It was the look of a predator closing in on its prey.

Stark had recovered enough to remain impassive, but he looked scared, just the same. "I might," he said hoarsely.

"Run the clip," DaLuge said to Sneed.

Once again, Daniel was unprepared for what he saw, and began to sorely wish that he'd paid closer attention to DaLuge on the way over. He watched the screen, amazed. What he was witnessing wasn't humanly possible! It had to be some sort of trick...a video dupe, a hologram...

What kind of hologram kills three dozen men in under a minute?

The clip wasn't very long, and when it was over he felt sick despite himself. Sneed had paused it on a frame that showed a soldier's head separating from his shoulders.

How did I miss all that? I was there!

The answer was obvious. He'd missed it because he'd been totally preoccupied with Maia.

He shivered, suddenly anxious. *What else have I missed?*

Stark, too, looked sick to his stomach, but there was something else there, as well...a wild gleam in the old man's eye. Was it triumph? Hatred? He couldn't tell, but he didn't much care for it.

"Why are you showing me this?" Stark demanded.

"Please, do not insult our intelligence," DaLuge replied. All trace of good humor had left his voice. "We know that you know something about this. It would help you to tell us the truth."

"Huh." The captive scientist barked a short, derisive laugh. "I might know something," he said, "but it wouldn't be what you wanted to hear. I've never seen anything – anything, you hear me? – that can do what I've just witnessed on that screen. So I have to assume one of two things: either your vid-feed was a dupe – which I'm assuming you've verified it wasn't – or you're dealing with something you've never seen before."

"So you claim to know nothing?"

The question hung in the still air. Through the window, Daniel could hear the surf against the bottom of the cliff, pounding away. Stark set his jaw and stared back at DaLuge for nearly a full minute, seeming to weigh his options. Finally, he said in a low voice, "I don't know what I just saw. But I had a friend once, name of Perdue." He swallowed hard, and Daniel saw the tears standing out in the man's eyes. He watched, fascinated, as Stark struggled to continue. "He...that is, I...he looked like that...person I just saw on that screen. So if that was him...well, I guess you guys killed him, didn't you? Blew him right off the edge of the mountain."

"That *thing*," DaLuge said coldly, "killed forty men. It might look human, but that would be impossible given the speed with which it moved. No human could move that fast. I may not know what it is, but I can rule out what it's not." He stopped, pursed his lips, seeming to think for a moment. "Whatever it is, it's obviously dangerous, wouldn't you agree?"

Stark didn't answer. He turned toward the window and folded his arms across his chest.

DaLuge studied him for a moment, then seemed to relax. "For some reason, I want to believe you when you say you don't know much about this. You seemed genuinely surprised." He took a deep breath, let it out in a long sigh. "Sneed? Have you seen to Mr. Stark's quarters?"

"Yes, sir. He's to be moved up to level eleven, topside."

"Level eleven!" Daniel spoke before he thought. "That's the same level as Mai..."

All heads in the room turned to look at him as he broke off. "As my, uh...massage appointment this afternoon," he continued, thinking quickly. "I could show him up there, if you like."

"Sounds good." Simon grinned and tipped him a wink. Daniel's face flamed, and he was glad DaLuge's next comment was directed at Stark. "I'll be needing to speak with you again, John," he said. "Probably in a couple of weeks. I'm nearing completion on a major project – I'm sure you understand. In the meantime, enjoy the view."

＊＊＊＊＊

No words were exchanged in the lift that bore them silently topside, and Daniel was relieved when they'd left Stark, locked up tight as a caged but comfortable rat in his new quarters. Randall had accompanied them, of course – no getting away from those damnable staring eyes, those twitching fingers. Daniel felt that if he didn't break away from the man soon, he might lose his mind.

He'd been more edgy than usual this week, and that was saying something. He felt nervous constantly, anxious about something he couldn't name.

"Will you be stopping by the young lady's room, then?" Randall's question held a subtle edge of facetiousness. "If so, I'll meet you later. I have some work to do."

Daniel swallowed his pride and pretended he hadn't just been insulted. "Yes, I'd like to stop and make sure she's comfortable."

Randall's mouth twitched with a small, secretive smile. "Very well then, sir. We'll meet later, at eighteen-hundred hours. We have a debriefing with Doctor DaLuge regarding this morning's meeting."

Daniel nodded, stopped in front of the door to Maia's suite. He watched Randall walk away, a well-oiled robot, his patent-leather shoes making no sound on the plush beige carpet. When the Agent had passed from view, he let out a deep sigh and relaxed a little.

He could have let himself in, but for some reason this felt like an invasion of privacy, so he knocked and waited. A few moments passed, and he was about to tap on the door again when she answered. Her voice seemed strained.

"Yes? Who is it?"

He answered in a low voice. "It's Daniel. I was hoping to...talk with you."

There was a moment of silence. "I'm...I'm not feeling very well this afternoon," she said. "Could you come back another time?"

A sort of exquisite anguish rose in Daniel's breast. "Can't I just speak with you for a few minutes?" His voice had risen into a plaintive whine, and it was all he could do not to just unlock the door, push it open and walk into the room. He controlled himself because he didn't want to frighten her; in fact, that was the last thing he needed.

"I..." she hesitated, seemed to consider.

"Please," he said, his voice cracking in desperation. "I need to talk to someone. I feel like I'm going out of my mind. I...trust you, Maia. I won't take much of your time, I promise." The weight of the words coming from his mouth seemed to pull from him a feeling, like a sigh, and he began to cry silently. Large tears splashed from his eyes, trickling down his cheeks and nose to drop without a sound to the carpet below.

Another moment of silence. "Well...all right." She sounded scared.

"Thank you, Maia." He keyed in the entry code and entered the room, wiping at his eyes, embarrassed by his emotional indiscretion.

She stood in the center of the room, arms wrapped around her chest. Her hair was pulled back in a ponytail and her eyes were large and seemed to accost him.

"Thank you," he said again, his voice low. "I...can we talk outside, where we did before? The view is...soothing."

✳✳✳✳✳

Maia allowed Daniel to open the sliding glass door to the patio, and stepped through behind him into the fresh spring air. The wind was cool, and she shivered, feeling a tiny stirring as she did, a glow of warmth through her abdomen.

She leaned on the railing. "How do you believe I can help you?"

He didn't answer at first, just planted his elbows on the rail, cupping his hands behind his head and staring at the greens and purples of the lush gardens below. From somewhere nearby, on the ground, muffled voices could be heard, then laughter. The sounds mingled with the distant roar of waves and the more immediate shush of the wind, sweeping Maia's mind clean.

I must be strong.

With the thought, a calm came over her, and she opened herself to the immediate situation.

He needs someone. This is an opportunity.

"It's all too much," he said, his voice low. "I...I'm expected to be something. I don't know what it is. I don't know who I am!" His eyes searched hers desperately. "Do you know who I am?"

The question was absurd, but something about his voice stilled her urge to laugh, or at least raise an eyebrow.

He really thinks I might answer that question!

"You're Daniel," she replied, keeping her voice calm. She regarded him with new eyes, feeling something like sympathy for him. *He's lost and desperate, poor thing.*

A sudden certainty overcame her.

I can help him.

She reached out a hand and laid it on his shoulder, and he shuddered at her touch. A long sigh escaped him, the sound as lonely as the wind across a high mountaintop. He broke down and began to weep.

"I'm...I'm afraid, Maia," he stammered, sobs wracking his body. His eyes held a feral gleam; he seemed so desperate, but there was a certain nobility there too, a pride...a wanting.

What does he want? The answer came almost immediately. *He wants to do the right thing.*

The realization swept her judgements, her rationales away, and she saw him the way only she could – the way she had seen Johnny the first night she'd met him.

Daniel's aura roiled with reds and blues and deep greens, and she gasped at it, for it was unlike any other she'd seen. There was an ancientness about him, a universality...he seemed in that moment godlike, a storehouse of all things human. His face was the face of a king, and she was drawn to him by an inexorable force she'd never before experienced.

I am a child of the universe!

Daniel gasped sharply as she opened to him, and she in turn gasped as the connection was redoubled. He seemed a veritable fountainhead of power, a juggernaut...she was terrified suddenly. She tried to withdraw her hand from his shoulder, but he'd grasped her wrist, his fingers digging in until it hurt.

What have I done?!

Panic threatened; the tiny life growing inside her seemed to turn and shift, low in her abdomen, and she heard a voice cry out in her mind as if awakened from a deep sleep. Daniel had stopped crying and stared at her with large eyes. He seemed to notice her pained expression and withdrew his hand suddenly, staring at it, then at her.

"What just happened?" he asked.

✻✻✻✻✻

She was breathing deeply, holding her wrist over her belly protectively. Her cheeks flamed, and Daniel thought in that moment that she'd never been more beautiful. And there was a glow about her, too...he'd noticed it when he first came in, but that had been before she'd touched his shoulder. Whatever she had done, her touch had cleansed his mind. The fear that had been holding him captive for days was gone. He felt sharpened; energetically fulfilled.

He spoke quietly, respectfully. "You're...pregnant, aren't you?"

Her eyes were huge and frightened. A small sound escaped the back of her throat, like a whine.

He kept his voice low. "It's all right. No one else needs to know, at least for now. I won't tell."

Maia relaxed a little, took a deep, shuddering breath, still staring at him. "I'm not sure what that was," she husked. "I...I can see your..." she trailed off, seeming uncertain.

"What? What can you see?" He reached towards her again, about to grasp her arm despite himself, and she recoiled. He stopped, abashed.

"I...I'm sorry, Maia."

"No, it's not your fault," she said. "Daniel, let me ask you something. What is this place – I mean, really? What sort of people are these, who hold me against my will, and have you all torn up to the point where you're such an emotional mess? And, if you're as conflicted as you say, then why don't you just leave? I...I would..." she swallowed hard. "I would go with you, if you wanted."

He turned towards her sharply. "You would?"

She returned his gaze, not speaking. He seemed to think for a moment, then sighed. "No. No, they would hunt me down, and they would kill you. These people have no morals, no qualms..." He shuddered, and for the first time, she saw that what he'd said was true. In his own way, he was as powerless as her. They were both simply pieces in a game.

An anger rose in her breast then, at the greed and thoughtlessness that could drive men to kill and manipulate this ruthlessly, with no thought or fear of recompense. She sorely wished Johnny were here, and not just because she was scared to death and carrying his child. It was this anger which had been his driving force. He would understand what she was feeling.

She held very still, calming herself internally. A sudden, welcome image arose in her mind, of Milos' smiling face. *We're coming for you, Maia.*

She surely hoped so. The thought of having her baby here, at this place, made her sick to her stomach. And, if Daniel was right and they found out about it, they might just eliminate her along with her child.

She decided to change the subject. "Have you checked on the little girl?" she asked. "My friend, Karla...is she still alive?"

He frowned, but he seemed relieved to talk about something else. "Her condition hasn't changed since she was brought in," he said. "As far as getting you down there to see her..." He shook his head. "It would be a security nightmare. We wouldn't get past two checkpoints without getting stopped. And then, to get to the medical level, there's a required level three medical clearance..." He stopped, laughed morosely. "Sorry. Don't mean to go on, but..."

"No, it's all right." She thought for a moment, then asked tentatively, "Are you feeling any better, by the way?"

He seemed surprised. "Well...yes, as a matter of fact, I am. I'm not sure what you did, but..."

"It's nothing."

He didn't seem to want to pursue the matter any further, and for a while they both simply stood there, wind blowing their hair and clothes around them, looking out at the cloud ships sailing the horizon above a turbulent sea. The silence was not particularly awkward; and, impossibly, Maia found herself enjoying Daniel's company.

Minutes passed. The sun slipped a little further toward its bed below the horizon, afternoon drifting towards evening.

"I don't know what you did," he said again. "But whatever it is, you obviously have a...a soothing effect on me, I guess. Do you suppose...would it be all right if I came to visit you again? Maybe tomorrow, or the next day."

"That would be all right." She had to stifle a laugh at the thought of this young man courting her, which is what he appeared to be doing...but if she had a friend in this place, he was it. At least he hadn't tried to force his affections on her. He seemed to defer to her in a way that suggested he regarded her with something like mystical adoration.

He drew a deep breath, blew it out in a long sigh. "I've taken enough of your time," he said. "I'll leave you now, and you can be sure I won't share your secret with anyone."

"Thank you, Daniel," she said, and the gratitude in her voice was real.

He smiled. "Anything I can do to help. And if I think of a way for you to visit your friend, I'll let you know." He reached a hand towards her shoulder, tentatively, and she allowed him to rest it lightly there for a moment before turning away. For a few moments she only stood there, relishing the view of light and shadow across the water, breathing deeply of the salt tang.

"I do appreciate it," she said, after a moment. "By the way – have you heard any news of my other friend, John? Is he all right?" She turned, but he wasn't there. "Daniel?"

The front door to the suite clicked shut, and she heard the bolt *snick* as it locked tight. He had walked back inside and left the room while her back was turned. "Dammit," she muttered under her breath, and sat heavily on one of the low-backed patio chairs.

She watched the ocean until the sun sank heavily beneath a cloud-addled horizon. When the first of the stars began to glow from the blackness, and the wind grew cold enough to make her uncomfortable in her thin cotton dress, she went inside and got a blanket off the bed. She took it back out to the patio and wrapped herself tightly in it, shivering against the wind but unwilling to go back inside, unwilling to let it beat her. Slowly, she grew warmer, until she could almost pretend that she was home, and happy.

For a while she thought of Johnny, and sadness tried to overtake her. But there was something new to fight for now. Johnny might be gone, but she carried within her body his living legacy, the evidence of his flesh made new and whole.

Under the stars, she slept, and dreamed.

Chapter 12

For Johnny Perdue, the past few days had become increasingly surreal. Time seemed to have completely lost its normal flow. Days stretched like elastic; nights burned into long eternities, in which he began to remember himself, to re-create himself as he never could have imagined. It was as if the journey was his own personal pilgrimage, a coming-home unlike any other in human history.

He was finding himself...but he wasn't sure if what he was finding was human any longer.

They'd been traveling for a few days; he wasn't sure how many, and he didn't care. With no physical body to concern him, he felt complete and free for the first time in his life. When he walked, he seemed to float, so much so that Esmerelda had commented on it.

"You're getting faster," she said. "And you're using almost no energy, which is good. Intent is everything, Johnny. Become the master of intent, and the dreaming body is an unlimited vehicle." She laughed. "Become the dream, Johnny. Reality is the illusion."

At times since Milos had reached into him, on the first day of their journey, he sensed his perceptions slipping. Suddenly, at the slightest provocation, the world would become a living net of light, consciousness exploding in every direction simultaneously. The world of objects seemed at these times nothing more than a reflection, pale images hiding the majesty of consciousness which resides in every living thing. He knew with his whole being that the seers were right – all things were made of the same basic energy...and that energy was itself conscious and alive.

This energy, they said, could be perceived, not with any sense organ but rather with the whole being, functioning as a single perceptual node in an infinite net of consciousness. Perceiving this energy showed seers the essence of things, and they saw that each living creature is made from the energy of awareness itself. Plants and animals were seen to have a glow about them, a unique aura that could be read by a seer.

"Maia is really the person who knows this area best," Milos said when Johnny asked about it, and laughed at the surprised look on his face. "What? As I've told you before, Maia is a powerful sorceress in her own right. She just doesn't remember her training...at least not yet. But she has a knack for shifting the world around her. You'll see."

"But how is that possible?" Johnny protested, knowing even as he did that the question was moot.

Milos just smiled. "If you were to really understand these matters as well as she, you'd be the most impressive being in the universe by now. Your density comes from your insistence in treating your body as if it is real, when in fact it is only your dreaming body and thus quite elastic. You can really do – or be – anything you can conceive of."

The thought was at once richly exciting and dully ominous, but he didn't dwell on it. His life was already strange enough. It seemed that he was gaining knowledge by sheer osmosis, and Milos and his companions seemed impressed.

Janet was mostly quiet and kept to herself, but Esmerelda had taken a special interest in Johnny, and traveled with him most of the second and third day of the journey. Her presence, much like Milos', seemed to shift something in him, and when he was with her, he found himself able to do things he hadn't dreamed of, with almost no thought and very little effort.

Only Martuk had failed to weigh in, but this was because he had mysteriously disappeared. It seemed that no one had seen him since the first night that Johnny had come to the camp, but when he asked Milos about it with mild concern, the seer reassured him with a shrug.

"Martuk is a dreamer of unequaled skill," he said. "If he were in trouble, I would know it. He'll be back soon."

"But if he's dreaming, then where is his body?" Johnny asked, to which Milos gave no reply.

Johnny didn't give the matter much thought, already having plenty to concern him. He was changing rapidly; he could feel it in every fiber of his newfound self. With the seemingly boundless energy of his new body came an indefinable itch to travel, to see everything, everywhere. After all, wasn't he invincible? An inner voice warned that there was still much to learn, and Milos and his companions were good teachers...weren't they? He felt lucky to have found them, but then...come to think of it, they'd found him, now hadn't they?

But to what purpose? What did they want with him? And then there was Maia. Certainly he must do everything he could to help her, and Milos had intimated that Johnny's role in her rescue might be pivotal.

Is that what they want from me?

It didn't matter; he would do anything to help Maia. But behind this desire lurked an unappealing question: what sort of relationship might the two of them have in the future? She had another life, apparently, that even she didn't fully understand, and he...well, he was a different person, now, wasn't he? And that was putting it mildly.

Ah, but these thoughts were useless. Best not to tax himself – indeed, it was best not to think of these things at all. It seemed that this brand of paranoid, hypercritical thought was the only thing that drained his energy. Whenever he tried to engage that part of his mind, he was left feeling weak, fearful and confused.

But when he didn't think...well, when he didn't think, he could do miracles.

✳✳✳✳✳

He'd spent some time each day experimenting, trying to find out what he was capable of. He found that as long as he didn't expend too much thought on any one thing, normal actions like walking and talking took almost no energy at all. His 'body' seemed to have a fairly normal effect on his surroundings. His boots kicked up puffs of dust when he walked, and he left tracks, though Esmerelda had noticed that they seemed to lose their shape much more quickly than anyone else's.

If he wanted to, he could pick up objects and move them around, but he had to stay firmly focused to accomplish this; if he lost focus, even for a moment, the object tumbled to the ground as if through thin air.

One afternoon, lagging behind the group, he'd stopped beside the slim game trail they were following. Taking off his shirt, he hung it over the limb of a stubby ponderosa pine, wondering what would happen to a garment that was only a dream.

At first he noticed nothing different, but when he looked away, distracted by the movement of a bird in a nearby tree, the shirt vanished. The next moment he found he was wearing it again, but it had changed color. He'd been wearing it for days, and it had always been a faded blue. Now it was a shade of washed-out rust.

His new companions noticed the change, and he asked Milos about it. "Oh, that's nothing," Milos said. "Since you are in your dreaming body, your appearance might shift and change quite often. Actually, I find it highly interesting that yours hasn't changed more during your time with us. Your physical appearance has been very consistent, so much so that I'm no longer surprised you were able to fool your friends for two months. Of course, you didn't know that you were fooling anyone. I imagine you must have thought yourself quite insane."

Johnny laughed, amazed that he could find such a thing funny. Now that he knew the truth of his situation, however, he could see the humor in it. It was another effect of the sorcerers' company on him, he knew. Fear was becoming a more and more abstract concept. Humor was the answer to many stressful thoughts – laugh and you could handle nearly anything.

At night, when the rest of the company slept in the open under blankets of clouds, with the high melody of starlight filtering down through the stratosphere, Johnny sat entranced, staring into the fire with eyes like glowing pits. For hours, it seemed that visions played before him, rippling with the coal-light. It was his own way of resting, dreaming within dreaming, but it was different than sleep. He was awake, no question.

What visions he had he couldn't say later. They simply weren't part of the continuity of his new life. But he always felt refreshed and renewed when morning came and his companions rose to their breakfast and a new day.

At times he found the visions too intense, and once or twice he started awake, feeling disjointed and split. It was as if his consciousness were in two places at once, looking at the fire with one set of eyes while another beheld a vision of a gigantic, luminous cavern that bustled and rustled with activity. A surge of fear always shook this second vision loose, and he would 'awaken' to find himself crouched, staring into the fire while Milos's snores rumbled through the early-morning dark.

One morning, Janet commented on the fact that the coals always seemed to last all night with Johnny there. "You are affecting the fire," she said. "Look at it, hot as hell and burning away. Did you feed it last night?"

Johnny admitted that he had not.

"Of course not," she said, eyes luminous. Her face split open in a rare, toothy grin. "You are creating with your perception. You fed the fire with your attention last night, so it accommodated you. What an amazing gift! Don't you see?"

"But I'm not doing anything!" Johnny protested. "Or at least I don't understand what it is that I'm doing."

"You only lack the proper motivation," Milos spoke up. "If your conviction is true, you are a deadly warrior. That's all you need to understand. Everything else is paper in the wind. Find your purpose, and nothing can stop you."

✳✳✳✳✳

It was Esmerelda who taught him to fly.

The sun was slipping towards twilight, and the two of them were out ahead of the others. She was the only one of them who could match Johnny's pace when he really felt like moving, and lately he'd really begun to feel it – it seemed that he couldn't travel quickly enough.

Not knowing the path, he followed her as she marched swiftly, seeming to barely touch the ground. Her movements were graceful and efficient, and he admired how little trace she left as she passed. He tried to mimic her movements, focusing his thoughts on the fact that his body was not solid, and was easily able to pass through several small bushes and trees without disrupting either the continuity of his 'body' experience or the foliage.

Esmerelda noticed what he was doing. "You're lucky," she said. Her eyes were dark pearls of laughter with no trace of envy. "You don't know what I would give to be able to do what you're doing. To turn your dreaming body on and off like that. You're like some sort of weird hologram."

She paused on a small rocky hillock, balanced on the edge of a small boulder, eyes smiling, large and round. Something in her gaze seemed to draw him in, and his perception of her form began to change around the edges, in his peripheral vision where he couldn't quite make it out. She seemed to shrink, to condense somehow.

Suddenly, she leapt from the rock, straight into the air – and then her compact form was gone into the glare of the sun, only her voice remaining, resounding inside his head.

Look up, Johnny! Up here!

A bird, much larger than a sparrow but with the same general features, flittered and flew in circles above his head, dancing on the gusting wind. It was speckled brown and white, and on its breast was a large, bright blue spot.

"Ez?!" He shouted aloud, and she answered, again in his mind: *You can do it too, Johnny! It's easy!*

He focused every drop, every ounce of himself, and felt the world turn around him like the tumblers in a lock. His body rippled and changed, pulses of arcing yellow-blue energy racing up his arms and legs. He felt it as an ecstasy that moved through him like fire, destroying all urge to resist.

He threw back his head and laughed like a child, then lifted off gracefully. He retained his human shape, though he knew he could change if he focused with enough intent. There was simply no need to be a bird or anything else, and he liked the feel of the body he'd been using. It felt like his own.

He rose slowly, feeling the air currents around and under him, imagining himself a leaf on the wind. The feeling was truly awesome. Something like a great sigh escaped him, a feeling of tension being released.

He began to experiment, doing slow circles and dives, following Esmerelda's lead as she swooped and twirled, bouncing on the breeze. Together they cruised the crowns of the trees, up and down the sides of the low hills through which they'd been traversing. Once or twice they rose high enough to break through the low blanket of clouds that hung like gauze over the afternoon.

All sense of time was suspended. It seemed that they traveled in a silently glowing realm of graceful curves and lines, swooping in and out of a perfect landscape, she a bird, he only a dream.

Traveling at the speed of the wind, all things are still.

He couldn't tell if the thought was his, Ez's, or came from somewhere else. It didn't matter. The experience itself was outside of time, outside of reality...and yet it was real.

A loud *squawwk!* tore through the vision, and he began to tumble. He sensed Esmerelda's instant fright as her bird form, cavorting in the breeze only a moment before, dove for the safety of the soil. She shifted sideways with a panicked flutter of wings to avoid the diving white blur that bore down on them, wings raked back, plumage shimmering, blinding them with the reflected light of the sun.

Johnny felt something in him let go, and a moment later he was on the ground, looking up, shaking and breathing hard. His body felt rock solid; breath was fire in his chest. Fearfully, he looked skyward, but Esmerelda's bird-form was gone. Only the white raven remained, albino feathers outlined magnificently against the sun, which had come out from behind the clouds during their brief encounter. With another loud screech, the bird flapped towards the protection of the trees on a nearby hill.

Before it got there, however, its body seemed to elongate and stretch in slow motion. Suddenly it lit up with a brilliant glow, and with a flash, it disappeared as if it had never been.

The afternoon was quiet.

Johnny stared at the sky where the white raven had been, expecting for a moment that it might reappear. It was familiar to him, that was the odd thing. He knew that bird...but hadn't that been only a dream? He laughed to himself. He was becoming accustomed to this particular conundrum.

"Don't mind me, I'll be fine." Esmerelda's voice was softly accusing, but her eyes held humor as she approached. She was holding her left bicep.

"Sorry. I think I've seen that bird somewhere, but I...hey, are you okay?"

"That was no ordinary bird," she replied. "And yes, I'm fine. It's only a flesh wound. Bitch got me in the wing." Gingerly she released her arm so that Johnny could see. Blood welled from the cut, but it was indeed shallow. Already it seemed to be congealing around the edges. Ez's eyes were bright.

"Milos warned me about that thing," she said solemnly. "He warned all of us. But I've never seen her until today. She usually leaves us alone." She looked at Johnny speculatively. "Huh. I wonder what she could want with us."

A strange feeling sunk through the space where Johnny's stomach should have been. "I know that bird, somehow," he said again, quietly. "I've seen her – I mean I've seen it – before. What do you think..."

But Esmerelda wasn't listening. She began to cast about, obviously looking for something. She disappeared for a few moments behind a small screen of bushes and then reappeared with some large, fresh leaves. These she applied to the cut on her arm, tying them in place with long stalks of sturdy grass which she clumsily braided together. "There," she said, plopping down on the damp earth. "That'll hold until the others get here. I think Janet has some unguent."

"So let me get this straight," Johnny said, squatting next to her on his boot-heels. "You were flying. You were a bird. And that other bird..."

"That wasn't a bird! I told you that!" she retorted.

"Right, right. But she – it – scratched you while you were a bird. And now you are yourself again, and your arm..."

"Bitch got me in the wing, already told you." Esmerelda leaned back, eyes closed. Her mouth curved up in a secretive smile. "The world is a very mysterious place, Johnny. Very mysterious. You should know that better than most." She yawned hugely and stretched out on the ground like an overgrown cat. "Gonna get some shut-eye now. Watch for the others. They'll be along soon."

*****

"What does she want with us?" Janet mused when Johnny had finished the story. "I've met her before, but only in the dreaming fields. She always keeps her distance. To attack Ez like that..."

"You said you knew her, Johnny. Do you remember anything?" Milos gazed at him intently.

Johnny could only shake his head. The truth was, his memories of the white raven were fragmented at best. All he knew was that the bird haunted him, and he understood why the others kept referring to it as 'she'. There was something markedly female about it. And hadn't it appeared to him as a woman the first time he'd seen it? Rising from the Mirror Pool like Isis, a writhing female nude with a shimmering body. Before she morphed into the white raven and flew away, she had sung a song of such exquisite beauty that he had been entranced, completely hypnotized.

He had forgotten until now...but how could that be?

He told the others what he had remembered. "I know there's more," he finished, "But I don't know what it is."

"You will remember in time," Milos said. "In the meantime, I'll tell you what I've already told the others. I've met the white raven many times, but only once in the waking world." He eyed Johnny somberly. "I saw her watching you on the upper plain, the day Maia was taken. I saw her, but I didn't want to believe it. I'm afraid she's got her eye on you, Johnny."

"But what *is* she?" Johnny asked, intrigued. "And what would she want with me?"

"She is a dreaming entity," Milos replied. "A conscious being that roams the dreaming fields and the waking world. In my experience these types are usually energy predators, and this one has shown no signs of being different. She's obviously quite dangerous, as evidenced by what happened to you and Esmerelda today. My advice is to avoid her at all costs." As an afterthought, he added with a rueful smile, "She's probably drawn to you for the same reason I am – because you're an anomaly. In all the waking world, you are the most like her, and she like you." He laughed, but the sound was a bit morose. "Two dreaming entities loose in the world at the same time! What are the odds?"

****

That night, while the company slumbered around him and he gazed the distances within the glow of the coals, J'hara the sleeper visited Johnny again, but not in the guise of the white raven.

When her opulent form arose from the coals, spinning into fire-trapped reality before Johnny's dreaming eyes, Milos groaned in his sleep and Ez cried out restlessly and turned over. Neither of them awakened, however, and a few moments later, both were more deeply asleep than before.

Jah-nee.

The voice was the call of a bird, eerily human, sounding in his mind like the chime of a very sweet bell.

Jah-neeee! Jah-neeee! More insistent the toll of the bell, more compelling the vibration that amplified his visions, stretching him to the horizon of the mind's eye and beyond.

Hypnotized, he could only watch with spiraling eyes as her form grew ever larger, more distinct. She was sickeningly beautiful, with sharp, slender features and dark hair that seemed to writhe and coil, shimmering through the heat like Medusa's snakes. He beheld her with something like reverence and fear as she reached out a glowing hand. Molten fire dripped from her fingertips, sizzling and popping when it touched the coals, which no longer glowed diffusely but now reached up with new hunger to embrace her like a lover.

"J'hara." He spoke her name out loud, relishing the feel of it in his mouth.

She smiled, her perfect 'o' of a mouth curving out and up in a smile. *Jah-nee,* he seemed to hear, echoing over and over through the caverns of his mind.

Jah-nee. I am here.

Chapter 13

"THERE IS MAGIC HERE," Milos said. His voice was solemn. "Can you feel it? We'll stay here, among the trees."

He motioned to a stand of somber spruce that formed a dark cove at the base of this last wave of hills, a stark uprising of earth that loomed forbiddingly above them. Higher up, it became the mountain range separating them from the coast.

"I have a feeling that tonight is the night that we put Johnny Perdue back together." Milos grinned and took off his hat, wiped at his face with his shirt sleeve. "Besides, the next few days are going to be tough on those of us with bodies to carry around. We can use the rest."

Someone had suggested that it might be wiser to continue on till dark, but no one pressed the issue any further. They began to set up camp. Soon a small, smokeless fire had been lit and dinner was on. Everyone tended to things with their usual efficiency, but the mood was not as festive as usual this evening...or it seemed that way to Johnny. The group seemed tired, though the end of their journey was unmistakably nearer.

Milos squatted beside the fire, hat tilted back on his head. His eyes were calm, belying the urgency all of them were beginning to feel.

Martuk still had not returned. The others didn't speak of it out loud, but over the past two or three days, Johnny had sensed an undercurrent of concern, especially from Esmerelda. Indeed, all of them had traveled more closely together for the past few days, since the incident with the white raven. There was a definite watchfulness that surrounded them now, and Johnny sensed something else, too – a trepidation towards himself...was it fear? Did they regret taking him in? He knew that they were right to be wary of the white raven, who was not a raven at all.

He'd seen the bird, watching him from a distance, a few times in the past few days, but always it flew away before he could get a good look at it. Once, it called out from its perch on a spiky pine across a small valley, and the whole company stopped, staring up in wonder. Its cry was primal and eerily human, seeming to echo his name from the treetops.

Jah-nee! Jah-nee!

"She is stalking you, Johnny," Milos said. "I would be very careful if I were you. These types are not to be trusted."

Johnny had nodded soberly, agreeing wholeheartedly, but there was something alluring about her, just the same. His nighttime visions beside the fire had grown strange and disturbing, and he suspected that Milos was right – the white raven was a dreaming entity that had found a way into the waking world, much as Johnny himself had. Now, for whatever reason, she seemed to be trying to contact him. She'd spoken to him through the fire, had given him strange visions that he couldn't remember during the day. He didn't know if it happened every night, but whoever she was, she was female and definitely trying to get his attention. And then there was the name

J'hara

that seemed imprinted on his awareness every time the cold light of morning brought him back to the waking world.

As a way to combat the growing sense of urgent trepidation which was the residue of such encounters, he set up a new challenge for himself – to appear and act as 'normal' as possible at all times.

He found that it really wasn't that difficult.

He helped around the camp as much as possible and made a point of physically touching and moving as many objects as possible. When his usefulness reached its limits, he would find a place to sit, close his eyes, and breathe. He knew this was not necessary, but the physical act of breathing seemed to focus him, bringing him as close as possible to a normal human experience. He seemed more solid after these meditations, more real; sometimes he even forgot for a time that he was different from those around him.

He traveled more slowly, too. Something in him dreaded the choice he knew awaited him.

What happens after? If we rescue Maia, what then?

It seemed a terrible thought, but it couldn't be avoided. He was getting used to the idea that he might be in this state for a long time, and certain brutal realities were pushing in on him.

He was only too happy to move at the same pace as the others, trailing Milos along the myriad faint game trails that Esmerelda was so good at spotting. The country they traveled through was beautiful, and he set himself to scrutinizing and memorizing every detail.

They'd been climbing steadily, though the grade was not steep, and the landscape had become more open, the view even more spectacular. Behind them, purple hills rolled away to the sunrise horizon. Ahead, the low coastal range of mountains loomed, separating them from their objective.

The vegetation had become more sparse and rugged, the air clearer and colder. Mornings, dew lay over everything, sparkling in the diamond air. At daybreak one morning, Johnny approached Milos as the seer stood on a boulder at the edge of camp, studying their back trail.

"Worried about being spotted?"

"No," Milos replied. "Not particularly. It's a grand vista, though, don't you think? It would be foolish to waste such a view without a moment for reflection."

"Agreed."

"You aren't concerned, are you?" Milos looked at him sidelong.

Johnny paused for a moment, considering. The truth was, he'd always been concerned. He'd always been watchful to the point of near-paranoia, but during the journey with Milos and his companions, he'd barely thought of it until this moment.

The thought disturbed him.

"No," he said. "I guess I'm not." He looked at Milos with round, watchful eyes. "Why do you suppose that is?"

Milos shrugged. "I would think that the influence of myself and my companions has something to do with it. You've had a lot to absorb in a relatively short amount of time – more pressing business, if you will. We don't seem concerned about detection, so you're not either."

"Why aren't you concerned?" Johnny was curious. "If we're spotted, patrols could be here in very short order."

Milos shrugged. "I don't know," he replied. "If you asked me how we avoid detection, I could hardly explain it. We move like the world around us. We don't show up because we don't exhibit the qualities of prey."

"Your bodies exude heat at a rate of ninety-eight degrees Fahrenheit, just like everyone else's," Johnny retorted. "They can scan for the human heat signature from orbit. If they wanted to find you, they could."

Milos laughed, but his eyes were cold as space. "No, they couldn't," he said softly. "If they tried, they would find nothing but air. Believe me, I've had my run-ins. Weapons and technology are no match for a lone sorcerer in his own country."

"But you're not alone. There are people who depend on you. I mean, just look what happened at the compound! It was shielded, about as well as it could have been, and they still found us. If that can happen...."

Milos had turned to face him. "Your people were sitting ducks," he said. "They were not warriors, and they did not die like warriors. They were good people, but in the end they were only prey."

Johnny felt something inside him go completely slack. Much as he hated to admit it, what the sorcerer said was the truth. There had been no strength in the compound's pitiful numbers, only a bigger target over their heads.

"You're right," he said, and his voice held the sadness that he felt.

The wind picked up, cold and clean, and he felt it as a vibration. Suddenly he wanted nothing more than to be here, in this moment, in his own body, feeling the wind....really feeling it with his skin, not this dream-vibration that rendered him less and less human with each passing day.

Milos seemed to sense his trouble. "Come," he said, and clapped Johnny on the shoulder. For a moment, Johnny could feel the other man's hand and he was grateful for the human connection it suggested. "Let's enjoy this beauty while we can," Milos said, pulling his cloak tight around his throat. "We'll be traveling again soon enough."

"True." Johnny gazed at the murky blue haze of hills. The view was intensified and sharpened by the sun; the daylight gained strength by the moment, and Milos' words stirred another question in him.

"Do you really know where Maia is?" he asked. "You said we were going after her, but you never said how you know where she is."

"I'm connected to her the way I always have been," Milos replied. "Through her dreams. I can feel her, I guess you might say; the way you might feel the contours of a stone on the bottom of a murky stream, using a long stick. You can't see the stone, but you know it's there. She is being held at a government facility near the coast, on the other side of these mountains."

"You know this for a fact?"

Milos simply looked at him with raised eyebrows, and Johnny didn't press the issue. After a moment the seer looked away again, taking in the distances. "I've been meaning to ask you about something," he said. "I've noticed that you seem more solid recently...I think you know what I mean. You haven't been exercising your dreaming body the way most people in your position might."

"Most people?" Johnny's voice was a bit angrier than he'd intended. "I thought you said I was an anomaly? I don't think 'most people' have been in this position, including yourself, so please..." he sighed and trailed off, unable to keep the anger going. As usual, Milos had nailed the truth. "I know what you mean," Johnny said after a moment. "After I found out how easy it is for me to fly, and then with what happened to Esmerelda..."

"You found out how easy it was, and yet you don't practice it now."

"I know. I know."

"In fact, it seems that you're making every effort to be as normal as possible. It is a unique challenge, and I think I understand it. When you spend this much time in the dreaming body, there must be a tremendous pull towards anything familiar."

"Yes!" Johnny replied. "Yes, that's exactly it!"

"When a dreamer exercises their dreaming body," Milos continued, "they always know that eventually they will return from the dreaming fields and re-enter their bodies and the waking world. This knowledge is a buffer against the unknown. If the dream gets too scary, they can just wake up."

"You, on the other hand, are dreaming in the waking world, a very difficult feat to begin with. I think that trying to act and appear as normal as possible is your buffer."

Johnny absorbed this for a moment. "I guess you're right," he said. "What I want most of all right now is to just feel like I'm really here. I have to help Maia."

"And you will. In fact, when we get to where Maia is...you're the one going in after her."

"I know. It makes sense. They can't kill me."

Milos studied him shrewdly. "You've already thought about it?"

Johnny shrugged. "No...not really. I guess you could say I just knew it would happen that way."

Milos nodded. "Your instincts are sharp, Johnny. How will you get inside?"

Johnny looked at him, surprised. "I don't know, actually. I hadn't thought about it. I guess I'll just walk in."

Milos laughed. "Now that would be entertaining. But I think we can manage something a little more subtle."

"How do you mean?"

"I mean that you will use a sorcerer's method to gain entry to the place where Maia is. You will travel as a seer travels."

"I'm not following you."

"A seer," Milos continued, "can use a variety of ways to move their consciousness. In fact, a seer doesn't even need to be fully asleep. I can do it sitting up." He said it with no trace of either self-consciousness or pride.

"You....move your consciousness?"

"It's a lot like dreaming," Milos said. "And you can do the same thing, but since you're already dreaming, your entire dreaming body can move, instead of merely shifting points of view."

"What are the ways you move?" Johnny was intrigued.

Milos shrugged. "That depends on the temperament of the person. I like water, myself. I sit beside a stream or pool and let my consciousness merge with the water. After that, it's easy. Water moves, I move with it."

"What about the others?" Milos had his full attention now.

"Janet gazes at clouds," the seer went on. "Ez you've witnessed yourself, shifting her shape and traveling on the air, as a bird. Martuk can travel with water, clouds, air, light...you name it. He's very versatile."

"Can you teach me?" Johnny asked.

Milos gazed at him calmly. His eyes were pools of light. "Think back," he said. His voice held a weird, shimmering quality. "You've probably already done it – we just have to figure out your personal predilection."

Johnny felt something probing his consciousness. A memory blinked into focus, instantaneously. He watched it play across his vision as if it was a video recording.

"What do you see?" Milos' voice came through a burst of static, as if he was on the other end of a hand-com.

I'm at Control, with Marshall.

Johnny wasn't sure if he was speaking aloud or only sending telepathically, but he was sure Milos could hear him.

He's working at one of the consoles. I think...I think he's working on the project to send someone to the City...they were still talking about it, even though I was too messed up to go. This....I remember this day, I think. It wasn't too long after I came back the first time. Oh wait, something's happening. Oh shit...I'm in the computer. I'm inside the compound computer system, no...no, the whole electrical grid. I'm inside it!

"All right, that's enough. Wake up, Johnny." Milos clapped his hands together, three times.

Johnny snapped back, head spinning. He looked at Milos, whose eyes were alight, face flushed. "Well?" the seer asked. "What happened?"

Johnny was excited. "I...I traveled just like you said. I went into the compound's electrical grid. It seemed like I could hear and see things that were happening in the compound. It was very odd...like I was simultaneously everywhere at once. Or, at least, everywhere with electricity."

"What happened? How did it end?"

Johnny frowned and thought for a moment. "I ended up out in the forest," he said after a moment. "Standing next to one of the compound's power nodes. They're like these mini power stations that—"

Milos waved a hand, cutting him off. "I know what you're talking about," he said. "I've seen them." He grinned, eyes shining. "Don't you see what this means?"

"I traveled, didn't I?" Johnny was still spinning from the sudden onslaught of memory, but he laughed just the same.

Milos grinned and whistled softly through his teeth. "Well, I'll be damned!" he said. "Maybe the modern world has something to offer, after all! I've never heard of a sorcerer traveling with electricity, but it makes sense. It's perfect, in fact."

"What do you mean?"

"The place where Maia is being held is a government installation of some sort – plenty of electricity there. You'll be in in no time."

Johnny smiled coldly. "I was never too worried about getting in," he said. "It's getting out that could be a problem. Maia has to come out the old fashioned way."

*****

Evening fell quickly, shadows deepening to full darkness, and the party huddled around the fire. Janet munched on strips of beef jerky, which she shredded methodically before chewing on them. Esmerelda lay in her hammock between two small trees nearby, eyes closed, humming to herself.

Milos and Johnny stood side by side, facing the fire. By stages, the sounds around them died. The wind stilled to a bare whisper of breeze. No one said anything, but a sense of expectancy grew among them. From high overhead, cold slivers knifed into the camp, remnant light from stars long dead or gone nova.

The fire was low and hot, coals glowing and snapping. A collective hush fell over the group.

"Look!" Janet said. The flames began to dance, higher and hotter, molten shades of green and purple twining between the glowing chunks of aspen that formed the base of the fire.

Suddenly a figure appeared as if from thin air, materializing in the space beyond the fire.

"Martuk!" Esmerelda leapt to embrace him. He looked younger than Johnny remembered him, and even more vibrant. Milos clapped Martuk on the back, and even the usually-stoic Janet looked obviously relieved that he'd arrived. All of them clamored to know where he had been.

Martuk's face was stoic as he bid them to sit, and only when they'd quieted did he begin. His voice was full and rich as he addressed Johnny.

"The night you arrived in our camp," he began, "After Milos had told you the truth about yourself, your consciousness faltered, and for a time you were pulled back into your body – although I'm sure you don't remember it. I followed; that is to say, I let my dreaming consciousness guide me to where your body lies."

A cold itch began to invade Johnny's senses, a blank numbness that pulled at him. Martuk's eyes seemed to bore into him, steadying and numbing him at the same time. "You, my friend, are in what we in the business would call a bit of a pickle." He assessed Johnny soberly. "Would you like to know the truth?"

"Which truth?" Johnny asked, suddenly very uneasy.

Martuk laughed. "The one about where your body is. I don't have to tell you, it's your choice."

A cold shiver crept up the space where Johnny's spine should have been. "I..." he hesitated, then shrugged. "Fuck it," he said. "Bring the truth. How bad could it be?"

Martuk nodded without smiling. "I like your attitude," he said. "So here it is. Your body is in a cave – actually, one of a series of caves, probably about six or eight hundred miles east of here. These caves are home to the creatures that have kidnapped you – or rather, your body, since you're here and accounted for."

"What...what sort of creatures?"

"They are humanoid, which leads me to to believe that they share a common ancestor with us," the old seer replied. "But that's beside the point."

"Why were you gone so long?" Esmerelda blurted suddenly.

The old man's face became sober. "A good question," he said. "They are sentient, as I said, and very intelligent. They have a queen; like a hive of insects. She is...well, ancient, for one thing, and incredibly powerful. Powerful in ways most human beings can't understand."

"But how do you know all this?" Johnny asked.

"I met her," the old man said with a grin. "You remember; you were there."

"What do they want with me?" Desperately Johnny pushed back at the crawling despair that threatened to drown his sanity, tried not to think of a certain house in a certain desert.

The fire cast a red-orange, haunted light around the clearing. Martuk suddenly seemed again the specter of an ancient man. His slash of a mouth leered around his few remaining teeth as he grinned ruefully, his white hair ensconcing his head like a wispy wreath. "I don't know," he said, voice hoarse and old. "They are far more powerful than I am. This time, I'm only the messenger."

Martuk sighed, and the sound was the most melancholy thing Johnny had ever heard. The fire glowed a milky blue color, then faded to green. The wind had slowed to almost nothing, and when the old man spoke again, his voice was low and gravelly.

"You may never awaken, Johnny," he said. "That is your lot, I'm afraid – to deal with your current state. I cannot tell you when or if you will be back to your former self. Regardless of anything else, the life that you knew is over. I'm sorry. But you do yet have power in the waking world. For whatever reason, this is their gift to you."

Johnny's mind reeled. "I might...never awaken?" he whispered. "Never?"

"It's possible," Milos spoke up. "But I wouldn't resign myself to that fate just yet." He regarded Johnny's distressed look. "Come now, young Perdue," he said gently. "Is it so bad? Like Martuk said, you have power yet. Will you squander it?"

Johnny clenched his hands into fists, feeling his nails bite into his palms, feeling his heart, beating too loudly, though he knew both were the products of habitual perception. "No," he said, and his voice was loud and clear. "No, I suppose you're right."

Martuk's face, wreathed in dying flame-light, was haggard and ancient. He looked tired suddenly beyond all reckoning, as if his body might just crumble into dust. The coals had burned down. "I must rest," he said, his voice cracked and hoarse. "Is my tent around here somewhere?"

Janet had already unfolded the piece of canvas and begun attaching rope lines to nearby trees. Johnny moved to help without thinking about it. His mind spun as he worked, trying to make sense of what the old seer had said.

I must be nuts, listening to him.

"I think you got it." Janet's voice was amused, and Johnny realized that he'd sunk one of the tent-pegs six inches or so into the hard-packed, stony earth, using only his bare hands. He hadn't even felt it. He straightened slowly to find them all watching him. Martuk approached, hobbling with his cane.

"Well, well," he said. "Pretty impressive, Johnny. Your focus has improved since I left. You're gaining in skill." He looked thoughtful. "You know, you should really try to appreciate your unique situation. You have almost unlimited time in which to develop your skills."

"Yes, and no control over my life," Johnny said sharply. "What happens if my body dies? Would I even know it?"

Martuk shrugged. "I don't know," he said. "If you want my opinion, you'd probably just blink out like a light. But you shouldn't worry about your body; it is in no danger...you just might not get it back for a while."

"If ever." Johnny's voice was bitter.

Martuk had hobbled around to the front of the makeshift tent and didn't answer. "I must rest," he said again, and all the force had gone from his voice. He disappeared into the tent, and soon they could hear his snores, a great sawing, rhythmic sound that was also somehow comforting.

Milos looked up from where he squatted by the remains of the fire. "We should all rest," he said quietly. "Like I said earlier, the next couple of days might be kind of rough. We have some climbing to do, and we're going to need every ounce of energy before this is over."

Soon everyone but Johnny was sleeping soundly. The wind had picked up a bit, and now it sighed through the sparse grass and broken trees, creating a soft melody to go with the snores of the campers. The moon came out overhead, half-full, staring down at the clearing below.

Johnny sat beside the fire, waiting for the visions, waiting for the dreamer to come to him in the flames. After a while, she did.

Soon, she whispered, and her voice was the voice of the wind through the forest. *Soon, Jah-nee. Soon we will be together.*

CHAPTER 14

LAZARO SOL sat behind his desk, eyes closed, counting silently to himself. His desk-com beeped at him for the second time, alerting him to the visitors waiting outside his office quarters. He ignored the beeping and continued counting. It seemed that everything was counting these days – counting his breaths, counting pills, counting the hours until he could leave this wretched body. He cursed himself for allowing the thing to get to this point, but it couldn't be helped. The Eldest had named him as steward of the boy Controller's body, and that meant he had to make it until solstice – only eight more days now. He wondered briefly if the Eldest had picked him for a darker reason – to force him to wait, to give his body more time in which to die naturally before Contact had been achieved. Was it a conspiracy? If so, he'd show them. He would not die. He would make it, and those who'd bet against him, if there were such, would be sorry they'd underestimated Lazaro Sol.

…two…three…four…

He exhaled, not liking the rattle in his chest. He inhaled again, drawing as deeply as he could without triggering a coughing fit

…five…six…

and then let all the air out, as far as he could.

…seven…eight…

He felt a little dizzy, but mentally centered, and when the desk-com beeped again, he slammed the 'transmit' key with exaggerated vigor. "Yes!" He roared. "Enter, and be damned!"

He punched the switch to momentarily unlock the outer airlock, glared balefully at the two people who entered, a man and woman dressed in white medical gear and green masks and gloves. "You're late."

"Very sorry, sir," the man said. The woman wheeled a small trolley cart toward his desk, upon which rode an assortment of tools and small gadgets. She didn't look up at him, concentrating instead on setting up an apparatus he recognized – a standard blood pressure cuff.

"I trust this business won't take long?" Lazaro rolled up the sleeve of his black robe.

The man had a shock of dark hair and a wide, reddened face with small eyes. Now he smiled, revealing yellowed teeth. "No, sir," he said. "Just a few standard tests to make sure you're well enough to travel. Earthside, isn't it? Sounds like a good time. Anyway, we have orders from a Doctor..." he picked up a clipboard from the trolley and flipped through it. "...Dr. DaLuge," he finished. "Your personal physician, I presume? He wanted us to take some tests..."

"I know about the tests he ordered," Lazaro growled. "You think you would be standing in this office if I didn't know what was going on? I would've blown you out the airlock without thinking twice about it."

He took a certain sick pleasure in the shocked look that came across the man's face, and was blessedly without further comment from him for the rest of the visit. He took a nice long look at the female tech's round derriere and the swell of her bosom before leaning back in his servo-chair, eyes closed again. During the ten minutes it took them to finish DaLuge's routine tests, he amused himself by thinking of various disgusting things he could do to her body, once he'd successfully commandeered Daniel's young and virile form.

Only eight days.

❋❋❋❋❋

The desk-com beeped, a remote call this time, and Lazaro Sol jerked awake. He'd fallen asleep sometime after the techs left. His mouth was dry, and there was a bitter, metallic taste there that he knew to be blood. He rinsed with the glass of fresh water that stood perpetually to hand, punched the key to admit the call.

It was Simon, looking frazzled and unkempt as usual, but with a certain air about him that immediately caught Lazaro's attention. "Hello, sir," DaLuge said. "Hope I'm not disturbing you, but I thought you'd want to know this."

"Yes? What?" His pet scientist was obviously excited about something. "Tell me it's good news for once, Simon."

"I should think so." DaLuge grinned, and Lazaro noticed something he hadn't seen at first.

"Simon..."

"Yes?"

"Are you smoking?" Lazaro almost laughed, it was so incongruous. DaLuge lifted the white tube to his lips, dragged, grinned again.

"Well...you could say that I'm celebrating." He puffed out a cloud of smoke, which was instantly sucked away by the Clifftop air control system. "You remember the problem I was having?"

"Oh, yes. Right. The, er, imaging something-or-other, wasn't it?"

"Imaging generators, yes."

"I remember you said you thought it could have been the major source of our problem. Have you solved it?"

"In a word? Yes. That is, I hope so. I have to run a few more simulations, but I think I nailed it."

"Wonderful, Simon! I knew you could do it."

"It was the girl," DaLuge continued, hardly noticing that his boss had spoken. He took another drag, jetted smoke from his nostrils.

"The girl?"

"The one the mosquitoes infected. We brought her in, you remember. I wanted to run some tests on her."

"And?"

"The secret is in her skin. She was infected by a rogue batch of our mosquitoes. They weren't ready, but they got out. And when they infected this poor girl, they gave us something quite interesting."

Lazaro felt the beginnings of the usual headache, but he knew better than to get in Simon's way when he got going on a really good explanation. Besides, it was interesting. He popped two aspirin in his mouth, washed them down, and set his glass back on the desk with a bang. "I assume you're going somewhere with this?"

"Of course." Simon grimaced. "The neural sequencers, instead of making their way to the brain like they were supposed to, set up shop in the first layer of tissue they encountered – her face and neck. The sequencers are programmed to insinuate themselves into the host's body, namely the neural tissue – we've used them for years, but the mosquitoes are a new delivery method."

"Simon –"

"Yes, yes, I'm getting to the point. So, normally the sequencers use neural tissue to replicate the program in the brain, but these little bastards are different. They made neural tissue – they used her dermal tissue and made it right there on her face and neck. I don't know how it happened, they're not supposed to be that smart. Maybe it was the organic component – you know, the mosquitoes. But the host's own brain is communicating with the new tissue."

A small pain flared up between Sol's eyes, and he closed them, mercifully shutting out DaLuge's animated face. "Simon, are you saying that she has neural tissue growing on the outside of her body?"

DaLuge took a deep, satisfying drag on the cigarette, dropped it and crushed it out under his heel. "That's exactly what I'm saying," he said, exhaling smoke in small rings.

"That's quite a trick, Simon," Lazaro said sardonically. "You learn that one in college?"

DaLuge ignored him. "It's got some very strange characteristics, too. It's like some weird hybrid. The synaptic activity in this tissue is off the charts."

"You're telling me that this girl is growing an extra brain on the side of her face?"

"Well...not quite. It's more like her brain is annexing the infected dermal tissue. Expanding its territory, so to speak."

"Ahh..." It was a concept he understood well. "So, how does this help you solve your problem?"

DaLuge pulled out a fresh cigarette and lit it with a deft flick of a small lighter. To Lazaro Sol, he looked like an old pro at the technique, and he wondered briefly just how long it had been since Simon had indulged this vice. He certainly seemed to be making up for lost time.

"Well, I tested a sample of the skin, and, like I said, it has some very strange characteristics, probably because of its hybrid nature. Electrical signals pass through it at a much higher rate than normal."

"Oh? That is interesting."

"Damn right it is," DaLuge continued. "So, I got Sneed to run all the specs from the batch of mosquitoes we lost, and I've replicated more of the stuff in the lab."

"This...new skin? What do you call it, exactly?"

"What?! I don't know! I don't have time to name it. But I think it's exactly what I need to fix the neural feedback loop I told you about. And here's the good part – I won't bore you with too many details, but I can implant it into the electrical suit..."

"Electrical suit?"

"We talked about this," DaLuge said, not trying very hard to mask his impatience. "You remember, I'm sure. The processing speed issue? The suit is necessary for buffering, but there was a discrepancy between the processing speed of the clone's brain vs. the speed of the rest of his nervous system. To put it in a nutshell, I believe the clone's brain, when activated, has been overpowering both the reaction speed of the suit and his own nervous system. The result would be something similar to the shutdowns we've seen in the first three attempts. Total meltdown, in other words."

"Of course."

"Anyway, I'm implanting the new skin into the suit. When the clone is activated, the neural tissue will be directly connected to his brain, and will allow us to use external stimulation to match the brain's processing speed. I'm telling you, this stuff is incredible. The new suit will be made almost entirely of it. He'll be quite literally wearing a coat of new, electric skin."

"Are you worried about compatibility issues?" Lazaro asked. "What if his system rejects the stuff?"

"Daniel is coming in for a physical next week," DaLuge replied. "I'm going to test him then for compatibility. I'll have to implant a small amount of the stuff in his own skin, see how it reacts. If it's okay – and I think it will be – then the suit won't be any problem either."

Lazaro grimaced. "So...what? You're growing this...this new skin in the lab?"

"As we speak. It's turning out just like the scar tissue on the girl's face – it's extremely durable stuff. We can blend it with a resin-polymer base and get something like a very elastic rubber."

"And it conducts electricity?"

Simon laughed. "Conducts? It does a lot more than that. Remember, it's neural tissue. Basically programmable, blank synaptic connections. Theoretically, as the suit is used, it will adapt and learn. It could be a great thing for the overall project, sir."

Lazaro smiled. "Ahh, Simon," he said. He sat back with a whirr of servos, his pain momentarily forgotten in the light of this small victory. "You've outdone yourself, as usual. I won't forget all this hard work – when this project is over, I'm going to make sure you get what you've earned."

DaLuge grinned ruefully, and a worried, introspective look blew across his sandy features. "I hope so," he said. He took a last drag and crushed out the butt between thumb and forefinger, wincing at the heat and blowing a stream of smoke from the side of his mouth. "I certainly do hope so."

Chapter 15

Daniel leaned on the brick wall that ran along the cliff's edge directly behind his room, staring out into nothingness. He was tired and felt grouchy and lonely. He'd finished the few small things he had to do, and had come out here simply to unplug, to detach himself from the sterility and boredom that were the hallmarks of this world...the Elders' world. He wondered if he might feel differently about things when he was made a full Elder.

He didn't think so.

He wished he could see Maia's balcony from here, but the view was blocked by apple trees and the curve of the building. It was just as well; if he could see her room from here, he'd never sleep. He thought momentarily about visiting her again, but he wasn't feeling very happy and couldn't think of anything clever or insightful to say to her. All the same, it was a sore temptation.

The breeze whipped at his hair and ears, and he closed his eyes, relishing the sensation. He wished it would really start to blow, to storm the way he knew it could here on the coast. He'd heard stories from one of the local techs, a toothy fellow with a lazy eye, about a storm the previous year in which an entire section of cliff, only four miles south, had crumbled into the sea.

"It probably won't happen here," the tech had said. "But can you imagine?"

Daniel *could* imagine it. He imagined it quite clearly, looking out at the horizon. Clouds skidded along the distant rim of water, but they were white and puffy – they didn't look like storm clouds.

I hope it storms. The thought came with an edge of anger. *I'll come right out here and watch it. And I hope it takes this place down with it.*

He sighed, disturbed by his own morbidity. A gull landed on the wall, only a few feet away, looking at him forlornly. It rocked back and forth on its feet for a moment, seeming agitated, then took off again with a screee!, wheeling into the breeze. He watched it for a moment, wishing he could grow a pair of wings. He wanted nothing more than to fly away, to escape into...into what? He didn't know. There was no avenue open to him. Whatever the Elders had planned for him, it was simply going to happen.

Nothing can stop it.

If it hadn't been for Maia, he might very well have gone completely insane. But there was something so soothing about her...her physical presence was like a balm to his senses. He'd been back to visit her four times in the last week, and with only three days remaining until his initiation, he felt that these visits were the only thing holding his fragile mind together.

Whatever had happened between them on the patio was strange; he'd heard of psychic phenomena, but this was the first instance in which he'd ever felt like he'd experienced it himself. The two of them had been connected in a way that was unprecedented for him. It was not sexual, that much was certain. Whatever it was, it was pure sharing. She had seemed to reach into the very depths of his being, calming him at a very deep level. And there had been a high level of intimacy, too; a part of him had simply known her secret truth, that of her pregnancy, without her ever saying a word.

His reaction to this knowledge might have been the most amazing part of the experience, for Daniel would ordinarily have been steaming with jealousy at the thought that she carried another man's child...but there was something so special about it, so natural and beautiful, that he could not bring himself to feel anything bad about it. This in itself was a kind of awakening, an epiphany. He began to see his jealousy for what it was – a bad pattern, a response to fear, something to be singled out and destroyed.

Conversely, the tiny life she carried within her body seemed something to be nurtured, protected from the schemes of Grandfather and the Elders. His feelings towards her, and hence towards her unborn child, were bordering on something like reverence, and at the thought that something might happen to her at the hands of one of Grandfather's minions, a red rage overtook him. He gripped the brick with both hands, so tightly that his knuckles turned white. His eyes shone to the horizon, a fanatical, deranged smile playing over his lips.

What is happening to me? Why do I care?

His mind seemed calmer, more detached when he was near her. The effect lingered for hours after he spent any time at all with her. Indeed, it seemed that her very presence was almost like a drug. He began to crave her – her voice, her eyes, her hair.

And, miracle of miracles...the visions seemed to have abated, at least temporarily. He was no longer beset by strange and terrible sights every time he closed his eyes, and as a result he'd been able to sleep much better this last week than he had for several months.

*****

During their last conversation, he'd told her of Mephisto Station and his life there.

"So you've spent your whole life in...space?" Her eyes were wide, mouth turned down in a puzzled frown.

"That's right."

"Didn't you have any friends? How did you spend your time?"

It was Daniel's turn to frown. "All of my memories of childhood are of study," he said. "Study and exercise. You could ask me anything you want about almost any subject, and I would probably have an answer for you. But I don't remember any friends."

He didn't tell her about Neana or any of the other young women in Grandfather's harem with whom he'd spent so many lust-filled nights. In fact, when he thought of these things now, they made him blush and feel awkward. He cleared his throat and began to say something to change the subject, but she was speaking. Her eyes were far away.

"I've always been something of a loner," she said, her voice soft and low, "but I can't imagine having no friends at all." Her eyes were kind and sad as she turned toward him. "I don't know how you could do it," she said. "It's all so..." she waved a hand vaguely in the air, at a loss for words.

"Cold?" He said, his voice touched by anger. "Sterile? These are the words that have been going through my mind lately. I can't believe I didn't see it sooner. I look around this place, I look out at this ocean, and I ask myself, why? Why any of it? I just want to go for a walk, but I can't even do that."

*****

A sudden slap, the sound of a leather shoe on flagstone, brought him out of memory-lull, and he pushed himself upright against the rock-brick wall, straightening in anticipation, knowing already who it was. Who else could it possibly be?

"Ah...sorry to bother you, young master." As always, Randall's false deference grated on his nerves.

"Yes?" He kept his face blank and his voice smooth.

"Did you remember your appointment with Dr. DaLuge?"

"My physical exam, yes, I know."

"So you're ready, then?"

Daniel let a little anger come through. "Dammit, man, I can handle myself! I don't need your constant baby-sitting! I'm not to meet DaLuge until fifteen hundred hours, and that's more than an hour from now. I'm pretty certain I can make it."

"With respect, young sir, I believe you may have lost track of the time. You have less than fifteen minutes." Randall's voice somehow irritated when it was meant to soothe.

Daniel glared at him, walked a few paces so he could see through the permaplast window to the chrono-readout next to the wallscreen. It read 14:48. He glared at Randall again, indignant that the little man should catch him this way, then dropped his shoulders and sighed. It would do no good to blow up here. Better to save the energy.

"Very well," he said. "I suppose you might as well lead the way, since I'm sure you're going to make damn sure I get there on time. Why do you suppose I need a physical, anyway?"

Randall smiled, eyes cold and distant. "I'm sure I don't know that, young sir," he said. He walked back through the condo and out the front door without a backward glance, and after a moment, Daniel followed.

✻✻✻✻✻

The exam was rudimentary enough. He entered a cool, clean white room with a chrome table and several cupboards and was asked to sit by the nurse who met him there, a young woman with cold blue eyes and very white hands.

He sat. He waited. Randall waited too, in the corner, looking quite at home next to a tray that held a variety of menacing-looking stainless steel tools.

He didn't have to wait very long. Simon DaLuge entered, looking fraggled and unkempt in this sterile environment. His brand-new white frock looked out of place, hanging on his gaunt frame. He pulled on a pair of gloves with a quick snap and smiled at Daniel.

"How are you feeling, Daniel?"

Like fucking hell is about to break loose, and no one can see it but me.

Of course, he didn't say this out loud. "Fine." He smiled back, wondering if DaLuge sensed his fakeness. "Been sleeping a little better."

"Oh? That's good, that's good. Well, as you know, you're here for a quick physical. We're going to run a few simple tests, nothing more serious than taping a few electrodes to your chest and forehead. Oh, and a shot."

"A shot? What for?"

For a split second DaLuge hesitated, and Daniel thought that he caught something there, a look...but the old scientist smiled and went on. "Standard multi-inoculation, brings you up to date for everything you haven't got yet. There've been several mutations of influenza lately that can be dangerous if not attended to."

Daniel laughed out loud. "So I'm here to get a flu shot?"

DaLuge looked puzzled. "More or less."

I'd bet it's more. A lot more.

"I assure you," DaLuge said smoothly, "It's a standard multi-inoculation."

"Whatever you say, doc. Bring it on." He laughed again, suddenly not caring what happened next. He was tired of fighting it, whatever it was. What would be, would be.

❄❄❄❄❄

The exam was over quickly, and he retired to the solitude and comfort of his room, knowing it was the only place on the grounds where he could be sure Randall wasn't watching him. And he wasn't even completely sure of that. For all he knew, there could be hidden listening devices all over his room and the small patch of lawn he'd begun to think of as his back yard.

He didn't care.

He flopped in one of the chairs on the flagstone patio, leaned back, listening to the eternal pound of surf on stone, far below. Eyes closed, he drifted, letting his mind wander. He wanted to go to Maia, to see her again, but something in him hesitated.

It's because you want her the way she was.

He opened his eyes, startled by this sudden insight.

It was true. She'd lost something when he took her from her home, some vital quality that had made her so beautiful to him in the first place. He could justify it any way he chose – he could pretend to be her savior, her rescuer, but that didn't change the fact that she'd been brutally ripped from her life, essentially imprisoned. That she could hold her head up at all, could look him in the eyes when he spoke to her, was in itself nothing short of a miracle. But she wasn't the same. She'd been injured in some deep way. He wondered if the damage was irreparable.

He hoped not.

He longed to see her again in her forest, to see the beauty of her face, alight with golden sunshine, filtering through boughs of fir and pine.

But not with the swarm. With my own eyes, my own body.

He would take her there. He could live with her there, in her forest, the two of them basking naked in the sun, living off the land, hunting and foraging. They could raise her child, could make more babies, could live in solitude, in peace...

The force of the idea was breathtaking, but he couldn't allow it to continue. He knew it was futile.

A terrible loneliness welled up within him as he put this dream to death, a sadness so permeant that it saturated him totally. His breath caught in his throat, and he seemed to feel a crushing pressure, a literal weight that pushed down on his chest so that he could barely breathe. A pitiful wail escaped his throat, the cry of a mewling animal, caught in a trap it can't see or understand.

He struggled to an upright sitting position, his breath a jagged wheeze. Blindly, he pushed himself up and staggered across the grass toward the brick wall. A trio of gulls flapped at him indignantly, then dove from the fence into the maw of the breeze. He reached the wall, clutched it with both hands, and threw up violently, hanging his head down the other side. He watched the trickle of vomit, running down into a crack between the bricks at the bottom of the wall, and lost his stomach again, with even more force this time.

Exhausted, he lay his head on the top of the bricks, relishing the coldness against his flushed face. He closed his eyes, felt the wind stir the short, bristly hairs on top of his head. A spatter of raindrop splashed against his closed eyelids, his ears, the back of his neck. He welcomed the sensation.

For a long time he stood like that, forcing back the futility of tears that wanted to come out, threatening to taint the purity of the rain-drenched moment with the stink of his own salt, the stench of his wretched life.

I am alone. Truly alone.

The thought ripped at him. Again he wanted to go see Maia, and again he fought down the temptation. He was tired of bowing to his rampant emotions; tired of feeling so needy; tired of being a pawn.

If I am alone, then so be it. It is what it is.

He drew a deep, cleansing breath, lifted his eyes to the cloud-riddled sky. Deep azure stared back at him, indifferent space. He breathed out, counted to ten and inhaled again, beginning the mantra that Maia had taught him.

I am a child of the universe. I am a being of light. The words calmed him, and he fought to gain focus, to remember the next part.

The power of light is the power of love.

Love? What is love?

Daniel didn't know. The mantra faltered in his mind, shimmered and faded, all but the second line. That one he could understand. Something about it made perfect sense.

I am a being of light.

He repeated it to himself, over and over, until his mind was utterly blank, a clean slate, a mirror reflecting only the slate-gray of the clouds that had begun to move in, the endless throb of water on rock, the susurrant stirrings of the air, the rustle of branches, the swoop and dive of the sea birds.

Before the sun had fully dropped beyond the edge of the world, he went back inside, exhausted, and fell into bed without bothering to get undressed.

He was asleep before his head touched the pillow.

✻✻✻✻✻

Rock and shadow blend, fusing into a surreal landscape, molten with pain. The heat is unbearable. Some substance, like magma, pools below, sending up silent gouts of orange steam in perpetual slow motion.

A movement catches his eye, and a figure comes into view. It is small, a child's figure, but how can this be? This child is old, bent and shriven, racked with pain. The fingers shake as with chronic palsy.

It is still hidden in shadow, but as it steps from behind the twisted rock escarpment, Daniel cries out in horror. Its face, lit with hellglow from the sulfur fires pooling all around, is a twisted mess. The eyes protrude at odd angles, the skin melted to show the bone below. From one ash-colored cheek, maggots squirm from rotting, pus-filled fissures, dropping to the ground, hissing and steaming as they encounter the smoking rock.

Daniel wants to run, but he cannot move. He is glued to the spot, his body responding in sickening slow motion to match the silent hell around him. Only the living corpse-child moves normally. It moves closer to him, dead eyes regarding him silently, and he sees that it is a girl.

"Who are you?" he asks, but he already knows. She remains silent. He licks his lips again. "What...is this?"

Her voice when she responds is a sigh, a ghost of a whisper. "This is my pain, my world," she says.

"You...live here?"

"I live in many worlds," she says. "All of them hurt. The bads got me."

"The bads. What do you mean?"

She doesn't answer, just stands there, and he thinks that if he has to stay here even a little longer he might lose his mind. She reaches out, touches his arm with her gray, shriveled hand, and a searing light smashes through him like a wave. The pain is beyond anything he could have imagined.

"We are connected now," she says with a sigh. "They gave you my skin. We're the same."

He recoils in horror, looks down at the backs of his hands. They're beginning to shrivel, to blacken. A tendril of smoke tails upward from a hole that's beginning to form on one of his knuckles. Oddly, though this place is the embodiment of pain, he cannot feel his body. His hands crumble to dust but there is no sensation. This is a different kind of torture.

"What can I do?" he asks, but his words have turned to mush, his face gone with the rest of his body. Only sheer will remains.

She is turning away, her body crumbling, but her horror-show face remains, its halloween grin leering at him. "You're the only one can help," she whispers, her voice echoing through his mind. "We're the same now. Only you can take my pain away. You can take it away."

✳✳✳✳✳

A long, terrible shriek awoke him, a howl of indescribable pain. Only after it had been going on for a few seconds did he realize that it was coming from him. His heart raced, pounding against his ribcage. The sheets on his bed were soaked with perspiration, which ran from his skin in small rivers.

His right bicep, where DaLuge had injected him with the 'flu shot', was throbbing horribly. It looked normal, if a little red, but it itched something fierce. He found himself scrabbling, scratching at it like an animal, still screaming at the top of his lungs. The itch grew, pulsing in him, through him, a nauseous vibration that ripped from him a fresh phalanx of terrified yells.

Was that real? Was I actually talking to that little girl? How could that be?

The dream, if it had been a dream, was too horrible for words. He screamed again, the sound reverberating through his small room, echoing through his ears, frying his mind. He screamed again, and then again, and again, but it was useless. He couldn't get it out. The image remained, staring from her private hell whether his eyes were open or closed.

A pounding sound began to hammer along with his heart, a throbbing that turned his vision to red-black smears. He howled and cried, trying to push away her crumbling, dead face, her haunted, staring eyes, the rasp of her voice like the wing of a locust over dry, dusty rock.

Voices yelled and carried on all around him, but he could not hear what they were saying. He didn't hear when the security team broke into his room, didn't see Randall leading them, eyes piercing and predatory. He didn't feel it when they injected him with his second shot of the day, a large dose of tranquilizer this time. He didn't feel the floor as it rose up to smash out his lights.

But he still heard the screaming.

CHAPTER 16

"I CAN SEE THE TOP!" Esmerelda's voice trilled through the morning air, joyous and bouncing. Johnny allowed himself a small flight of fancy and elevated quickly, coming to rest atop an impossibly tall pine. The topmost spire of the tree rustled and bent as if it knew there was something there, but his body was light as air. He perched there like some oversized bird, looking over the top of the ridge at the falling waves of hills that meandered westward. In the distance, a line of clouds at the horizon's edge spoke of the sea.

"Can you smell it?" Ez yelled up at him. "I can smell the ocean!"

He closed his eyes and inhaled deeply, willing himself to feel the air, to catch odors like he sometimes could. Something deep in himself opened like a lock, and for the briefest moment he did smell it, the tang of salt on the skittering breeze. He grinned down at her.

Even though the climb had been easy for him, he was glad it was over. More than glad, in fact; a pinnacle had been reached, and he wasn't the only one who felt it.

It's all downhill from here.

Milos pushed up to the ridge-top, stopped and took off his hat, using it to fan his face. "Well now!" he said brightly. "That's a nice sight."

A small clearing in the trees marked the downslope to the west, and the view was spectacular. At the very edge of the world, battalions of clouds marched in dark, misty cadence. The sea was not visible, but they all knew it was there, just the same. A few gulls wheeled in the near distance, and the vegetation had changed, too. The plants were hardier, the trees scrubbier.

Johnny floated to the ground and landed beside Janet, who had just arrived. She took off her pack and stretched, then got out a small flask of water and the last of the jerked venison and passed it around without a word.

"Where's Martuk?" Johnny asked.

As if on cue, the old sorcerer stepped out from behind a nearby tree. Of them all, he looked the most unperturbed by the climb, and Johnny was struck by the question of how the most ancient among them should be able to travel at all, much less climb mountains, without seeming even to break a sweat.

"Right here, youngster." Martuk's smile was dazzling. His body looked more youthful than Johnny had yet seen it; his hair seemed to have lost all its gray, and was now a rich, luxuriant black. It seemed to have been recently combed. His face was clean. His walking stick and the small pack he carried were nowhere in sight, and stranger still, he was dressed in expensive modern clothing; a loose-weave cotton shirt and dark brown slacks, and shiny patent-leather shoes. He looked every bit the modern man, not a day over forty.

The sight was so incongruous that Johnny gaped, then turned to Milos, who guffawed and slapped his knee in an exaggerated gesture. Martuk grinned. "The world is a trick of perception," he said. "You amaze too easily."

"Especially for someone who thinks nothing of flying around like Peter Pan," Janet said gruffly.

Johnny laughed. "I suppose you're right," he said. "I should be used to it by now."

The mood was light, almost festive. The hardest part of the journey was over, and Ez was right; this was sea air they were breathing. It was intoxicating, even for Johnny.

"How far, do you think?" Janet asked.

Milos took off his hat, scratched his head and squinted at the horizon. "No more than a day and a half, I should think." He frowned. "I don't know why, but I have a feeling that we're more pressed for time than we thought. Any objections to going on till dark?"

✳✳✳✳✳

Martuk retired with the setting sun that night. "I must plumb the dreaming fields," he remarked cryptically, his voice again cracked and old. "I must scout the rest of our journey. We are close, though – very close." He ducked his wizened form beneath the flap and into the darkness of his tent.

Janet set about finding more firewood as Esmerelda squatted beside the fire, feeding its hungry, snapping jaws with small dry twigs and pine cones.

Johnny floated up to a small, rocky outcropping above their camp, coming to rest on a small earthen shelf in the rock. Above him, hardy scrub pine clung to life, bravely turning wind-blasted boughs to the west, toward the scourge of the elements that had carved this place.

He peered at the horizon, noticing that the clarity of his sight became telescopically better the more he focused on it. In the distance, his new vision caught the glitter of light on water.

"I can see the ocean!" he called down to Milos, who looked up from twenty feet below.

"That doesn't surprise me," the sorcerer remarked. "We should be no more than a few miles away from it." His voice was suddenly very close, too close, and Johnny turned to find the older man sitting comfortably next to him on the shelf of rock.

He gasped, at which Milos began to laugh uncontrollably, shaking rhythmically. He clapped his hands together. "Whoopee!" he cried. "I've succeeded in astounding the peerless dreamer yet again!"

"How did you do that?" Johnny asked, incredulous.

"The waking world isn't all that different from the dreaming fields," Milos replied. "It's all about correct use of available energy. And there's a lot available if you know what to look for." He yawned and stretched, then shaded his eyes against the setting sun, looking to the west. "Damn!" he said. "If you can see the ocean, your eyes're better than mine. But then, look who I'm talking to. You could probably see all the way to Mars if you focused hard enough."

Johnny was fascinated. "You really think so?"

Milos shrugged. "Who knows? The dreaming body is a very mysterious thing, and yours is being manifested, facilitated somehow by an incredibly powerful source. If Martuk is right – and I assure you that he probably is – then your physical body is being changed, too, at a cellular level." He peered at Johnny, who visibly shivered.

Milos laughed again, and Johnny glared at him. "It's not funny to me," he said gruffly. "I don't think it would be to you, either, if it was your body."

"I wasn't laughing at you," Milos explained. "But it was funny when you shivered. Your physical reactions are so dead-on...you're the consummate actor. You're so good, sometimes I forget that you're dreaming. That's what makes you the peerless dreamer."

"Thanks...I guess. But I don't really feel like I'm doing anything."

Johnny reached out absently with his right hand, plucked a large pine cone from a small tree at least five feet above his head. He tossed it over the side. It plunked down the hill, bounced and rolled next to Esmerelda, who promptly pulled it apart and fed it to the fire without looking up.

Milos shook his head. "Amazing! Do you even know what you just did?"

"What are you talking about?" Johnny was in no mood for games. "Since you're up here, can I ask you a question?"

Milos raised an eyebrow. "What is it?"

Johnny stared straight ahead, into an uncertain future, and sighed. "What happens after we rescue Maia? For me, I mean. I assume the rest of you will move on to wherever you're going next, and from what you've told me I'm pretty sure she'll go with you."

Milos sighed. His eyes were kind but somber. "And you want to know where that leaves you."

"Exactly."

Milos thought for a moment. "You could come with us if you want," he ventured. "You fit right in with this troop of crazies."

"Yeah." Johnny pondered for a moment. "Yeah, I guess so." His tone suggested that he felt otherwise.

"No?" Milos raised an eyebrow.

"Well...Maia and I have a history. I...I loved her, you know? I still do love her, but it's different now. I mean, I don't have a body. I don't sleep. I don't eat, I don't feel the wind or the rain unless I really try hard, and even then I'm not sure if it's the real thing or not. I don't go to the bathroom. I'm a freak. I can't expect her to feel the same as before."

"If anyone could understand," Milos said kindly, "It would be Maia. But she has remembering of her own to do." He looked thoughtful. "Perhaps seeing you could be the catalyst; the event that could re-align her memories. And that would be a very good thing."

Johnny was suddenly, acutely aware of a somewhat painful and surprising fact: Milos and his group had a very specific agenda of their own, which was more important to them than any one person or ideal. They were refined, not brutish, but he had a feeling they would allow little to stand in the way of their goals. Freeing Maia, he knew, was only the first step.

Milos seemed to sense where Johnny's train of thought had derailed. He grinned sheepishly. "Sorry," he said. "Just speculating." He drew in a deep breath, pursed his lips, let it out in a whoosh. "To tell you the truth," he said, scratching his head, "you're probably right – about things not being the same between you and Maia. We could go round and round on the subject, but I prefer to react like a warrior."

"And how is that?"

"Action, not speculation," Milos answered promptly. "Action without fear, measured against known facts. You must deal with events as they arise. It's difficult to predict how she will react to you." The seer's face was calm and kind. "As I said, my way is the way of the warrior. There is no time to think of what cannot be changed. There is only ever time to do. Or don't – either way is the same." His words seemed both sad and profound to Johnny.

They fell silent. Further down the ridge, where the evening sunlight touched the tops of the pines, a flash of silvery white caught them at the same time, the shine of sunlight on iridescent feathers. A cry resounded, eerie and familiar.

Jah-nee....! Jahhh-neee...!

The bird's preternatural cry tailed off into the echoing lament of a screaming violin, sad and vulnerable.

Johnny shivered, and for the briefest moment the gooseflesh that rose on his arms was real, not simply a projection. Something stirred inside him, a resonance that coalesced a feeling he hadn't known in a very long time – a pure passion that tingled through him like electricity.

Milos' words were tinged with regret. "She is stalking you," he said, his eyes sweeping Johnny with concern. "And she's doing an effective job, from the look of it. She will make her play for you soon."

The bird was gone again, but its cry still echoed through the trees.

Down below, Esmerelda peered up into the darkening twilight anxiously. "Would you two stop stirring up trouble?" she said crossly.

"And what do you think about it?" Johnny asked Milos.

"About what, exactly?"

"Will she get what she wants? Will I go with her?"

"Ah." Milos' face was sad. "At least you know what you're up against. Because that *is* what she wants. To her, you represent a power source unequalled in all the dreaming fields. If she had you all to herself..."

"You didn't answer my question," Johnny interrupted. "What do you think I will do?"

Milos studied him for a long moment. "You'll go," he replied calmly. "In the end, I think she will succeed. She knows your weak spots. Despite your knowledge of what she's doing, there is something about her that you love, something you can't get enough of."

Johnny took a deep breath. "Thank you," he said. "For telling the truth. I don't know if you're right, but I needed to hear what you thought."

"No problem." Milos grinned widely, then launched from their shelf of rock with no warning, landing with apparent ease, like a cat, on all fours. The dirt under him barely stirred, though the distance was more than twenty feet. He stood up and grinned at Johnny, who floated down, still sitting in the lotus position, and came to rest on a log that Janet had pulled up next the fire and was using as a combination bench and table.

Milos dusted himself off with his hat. "Showoff," he said in a disgusted tone. "You make me sick."

✳✳✳✳✳

The night was cool but humid; the scent of rain was in the air.

They were close, that much was sure. "Have you given any more thought to what we talked about the other night?" Milos asked as the fire burned down.

"You mean about storming the castle?" Johnny said with a smile, but no one laughed at the joke. Milos didn't say anything, just poked casually at the coals with a long stick. His eyes, however, were anything but casual as they watched him.

Johnny didn't reply for a moment, and when he did, they all listened with rapt attention. "Well, I've thought of just flying in, but they'll see me and all hell would break loose. It might be hard to get Maia out of there under those conditions. I think stealth is a better option."

There were murmurs of assent from Milos and Janet. Esmerelda rocked slowly in her hammock between two small trees, legs dangling, looking pensive and vulnerable as any young girl might. She was biting her lip, a troubled look on her face.

"What Milos said, about using a sorcerer's method to travel, sounds like it might work," Johnny continued. "I don't know if he told the rest of you, but apparently I've used electricity to travel in the past, though I didn't know then what I was doing. I think now I'd have a better idea. If I could have some control over where I popped out on the inside, I would stand a good chance of remaining undetected, so long as no one sees me. Then I find Maia and get her the hell out of there."

He looked around, thinking that the sheer brazen insanity of the thing was appalling to say the least, but they were nodding agreement. "Traveling by electricity," Janet said, her voice filled with awe. "That's a new one on me. Even by sorcerer's standards, it seems risky."

"I've done it before," Johnny said grimly, with more resolve than he felt. "The hard part is finding a place to get in – a power line, a transformer grid...anywhere that power goes into or out of the place. There has to be a mainline, a power station, something...and we have to find it without getting caught." He looked around urgently. "I know you're all capable of protecting yourselves, in ways I still can't understand, but please — be careful! We can't run the risk of underestimating these people or their zeal to protect themselves. Security is probably an obsessive issue with them."

For once, Milos did not make light of the situation. His eyes were calm and deadly, storm clouds building there on a near horizon. "We will not make that mistake, you can be sure," he said. "As for your plan, I think it's a good one. Bold and cunning – the plan of a warrior. And you're making use of your gifts to their full extent. I wish you'd had some time to gain experience with this method of travel, but it is certainly possible within the realm of what we know. I myself have traveled far in my dreaming body, both with cloud and water, two natural elements. Electricity is no less natural, and it certainly does travel."

"Well," Johnny said, "if it doesn't work, I'll go back to the first plan. Fly in, locate her, pull her out. Either way, it's going to be hard for them to kill a guy with no body."

Janet laughed, then Milos joined in. Even Esmerelda, glum and watchful only a little while before, looked happy and relieved. Johnny looked around, feeling their smiles, and took a mental snapshot of each of them. Something told him that, as a group, they might not have much time left together.

As if reading his thoughts, Milos said, "We should sleep soon. Tomorrow could be a very long day."

CHAPTER 17

The night was quiet and spooky. Moonlight played between dark, ribbed clouds, limning the undersides of the leaves on nearby trees with an unearthly silver glow.

Johnny was not tired, nor did he feel like fire-gazing this night. He felt strong, full of nocturnal energy. And he felt like being by himself.

He left Milos and company sleeping beside the fire, levitated a couple of feet and floated like a feather between the trunks of the trees, away from the camp, angling towards the coast. The night was bright – the moon had come out from behind the clouds and now cast a milky pall over the forest.

Rocks thrust sharp edges toward the sky, knife-edged and forbidding. Bent and twisted pine trees flaunted many-fingered boughs, each needle visible in the dreamlight. Grass and ferns grew in the hollows between the trees, blades of green turned black by the night. Details stood out in sharp relief, to the point where sometimes he was convinced that his dreaming imagination was filling in the blanks, providing his ever-questing mind with more than was really there.

There's no difference. It's all energy and the perception of energy, awake or dreaming. You see with your mind, not your eyes.

He startled an owl sitting on a lightning-blasted snag, and it took off with a dark flapping of shadowed wings, hooting indignantly. He laughed and kept going, wondering exactly what it saw when it saw him. A person? A ghost? Some sort of presence?

He couldn't begin to guess.

None of his old fears were in play any longer. Bears and mountain lions were no longer a danger – he couldn't be killed by any of the night-time predators one might fear in the wilderness. He couldn't starve, or drown, or freeze to death. He couldn't be tracked by normal satellite recon, either. He was seemingly untouchable. The fertile night was his to enjoy, to wander through as he saw fit.

Alone. With no body to feel the night air, no need for rest, or shade, or water, or sleep. The peerless dreamer.

A bitter melancholy stole through his heart, a slow dance of exquisite pain that worked a cold spike through the deepest part of him.

I am alone in the night. There is nothing like me, anywhere.

Somewhere far away, a dog howled, or perhaps it was a coyote. The sound was as lonely, as melancholy as his thoughts.

He shook off the feeling angrily, knowing there was no use indulging such thoughts. As Milos might say – take action, don't speculate. Besides, what was there to worry about?

Only the most unlikely of foes.

He wasn't worried about rescuing Maia. He knew that he could get her out, probably with very little trouble. Now that he knew who he was and what he could do, he would be unstoppable.

But what then? He loved her; he knew she loved him. But the problem obviously extended far beyond concerns of romance, for how could they possibly be together? If Milos was right, then Maia would soon remember herself, her time spent with the sorcerers...a whole other life. She was going to have a lot to do, and to deal with.

And where would that leave Johnny? Not necessarily out of the picture, but then, the picture had changed, hadn't it?

It was boredom, then, that was his enemy, that most unlikely of foes...but he had to contend with it.

Without normal survival concerns, the question became – what to do with his time? He didn't appear to have a choice regarding his being here, in quasi-human form, in the waking world.

He wondered if he would ever again see this world through his own two physical eyes, or if he was destined to wander the purgatory between the dreaming fields and the waking world forever, neither ghost nor human, but something else. Something *other.*

Lately, a certain thought had occurred to him, and it was a thought he liked, because it meant action. A way to fight the boredom.

*****

The idea had come from a conversation with Marshall Scott and John Stark, during an afternoon spent in Control, a few months after he'd arrived at Compound West.

Before we went to the Falls. Before the mosquitoes, even.

They'd been looking over the pirated data from the disk that had been Johnny's original reason for leaving Montana Compound in the first place.

Stark had been analyzing a string of satellite images showing a section of City 7, the closest metropolis to the north. He'd been quite animated about pointing out some incongruities he'd noticed. "You see here," he said. "This is an old rail yard. They used to run trains through there before the War. See the stacked railcars?"

"What about it?" Scott replied.

"This whole area is in what they call the Rim - the area outside the city proper where supposedly the only people are the vagrants - the rat culture, you know. But here..." he pointed with the tip of his pencil, "...here, everyday for at least two months running, you can see something that resembles an organized watch. This building here..." the pencil tapped the screen on the right side, "...this building is an old office. It should've been gutted, overrun by looters and the like, but you can see here that it's been cleaned up and made more defensible. And here..." he clicked to the next image, "...and here..." Another image, then another. "In all these shots you can see a constant but predictable rotation of...well, personnel, I guess you'd call them. A lot of the same people, or at least people who look the same from this angle."

"What does this mean?" Johnny asked, intrigued.

Stark looked up at him shrewdly. "Well, it means organization. And if there's an organized group...well, they're clearly not government sanctioned, if you know what I mean."

"They'd make natural allies," Johnny said, seeing the importance of this fact immediately. "If they've survived, they must have a level of sophistication. Like us, and all this..." he gestured to the anti-surveillance equipment that surrounded them, the very guts of Control.

"Right. Right." Stark's eyes were far away, speculating. "And who knows...? Maybe we should try to contact them."

*****

The conversation had drifted to other things after that, and they'd never really discussed the issue again. Shortly thereafter, life in Compound West had gotten considerably more difficult, and Johnny had barely thought of the subject since then.

But now...

Things are different now, that's for sure.

Why not go north, try to find these people, if they existed? An underground society would be a society at odds with the government, and that meant they would be friendly to anyone who opposed that government. And he certainly fit that category.

Why not, indeed.

All his life, Johnny Perdue had wanted to do something real. To make a difference, to strike a blow against the bastards who'd killed his parents. These were the same bastards who'd killed everyone at Compound West.

He recalled what he'd done to that platoon of soldiers on the sun-drenched clifftop, the morning that Maia had been taken, and shivered with an electric chill that was almost pleasurable. The scene played out in grisly detail in his mind's eye, and the power that went along with that searing violence was all but impossible to deny.

He shuddered with the feeling, the killing heat that rose in his chest. He let it in, let it pool, then reached out with it, pointed it at the bole of a nearby tree, a medium-sized knotty pine, maybe most of a foot through the thickest part. He let the rage build for a moment longer, then attacked the tree with his whole being, flying towards it in a blur, smashing through it with his hand.

It snapped like it had been hit by lightning. The top two-thirds of it, twelve feet or more, fell with a series of cracks, thumping to the carpeted forest floor in a small shower of needles.

Johnny laughed out loud in the ensuing silence, an echoing shriek that would have sounded mad to a casual observer.

I could go after them, whoever they are. I'd be fucking unstoppable. I could wreck them all! I –

Unexpectedly, he broke through the tree-line and into a grassy space, windswept but not barren. Trees grew here, and sawgrass, moving in the breeze. Without being conscious of it, he touched down and began to walk through the swishing grass, arms at his sides. He could hear the ocean now, he realized; had been able to hear it for a few minutes, in fact, though he hadn't noticed.

The night was pregnant with expectation. The orb of the moon was huge overhead, nearly full. It swelled until it seemed to nearly fill his field of vision, painting the grass and bushes with a cool white light. The purple-blue night around him seemed suddenly haunted, magical, its consistency like that of crushed velvet. Trees seemed aware, turning toward him as he approached, half walking, half floating, senses entwined with the night like a lover, eyes wide open. From ahead and below, the crash of waves on rock was hypnotic.

He reached the edge of the cliff almost before he had noticed that he was coming to it, a dark line against the blue-black of the overcast horizon. The view was spectacular. The coast stretched away below him to the left and the right, a dark, windblown landscape, alive in the moonlight. Far to the north he saw a cluster of lights above the shoreline and wondered if it was part of a city, or perhaps the place where Maia was. He thought it more likely the latter, and played with the temptation to go there now, to try to find her tonight...but he knew that wouldn't be the wisest choice.

Instead, he focused on what he could see from his lonely clifftop vista. This was, after all, the first time he'd ever been to the ocean.

The horizon was dark with a line of clouds, but the moonlight gave shape to the near distance. The ocean seen from this height seemed peaceful, a gray mass that writhed rhythmically to the beat of earth and moon. The sound, too, was soothing. For a long time he stayed there, taking it all in, listening to the song of the surf and the occasional screech of a solitary gull, making its way north, tacking into the wind below him.

Overhead, clouds moved with the coastal wind, streaming ceaselessly.

He looked down.

Perhaps three hundred feet below, stretching away to his left, white crescents of foam formed, dissipated, re-formed as waves, rolling against white sand beaches. There was something so beautiful about the scene that it tugged at him. He wanted to be part of it.

Before he could think twice about it, he dove from the cliff's edge, into the rising wind, letting go completely, free falling. Fear seemed a distant thing, the puzzling choice of a confused person.

The rush of air on his face was tremendous, nearly real. He plummeted like a stone, faster than a stone, toward the crashing waves, their roar echoing and redoubling. Fifty feet above the ground he swooped like a bird, out over the water.

Beneath him, white-crested waves crashed against rocky cliffs. In the moonlight, the foam seemed to glow, or maybe it was his own awareness, which was tremendously heightened. The world had taken on a crystalline quality; he seemed to have entered a state of super-reality.

Time slowed.

The energy of the ocean was tremendous, and he felt something deep in himself resonate with the crushing mass of the water, the life-giving sea. Its evolutionary pattern was set deep in the tides of his blood, the calcium reef that was his bones. Even though that body was far from here, he saw it all in full detail...but he missed the feel of wind and water, sand and stone against his skin.

He longed for his body suddenly, would have gladly traded in the ability to fly, the ability to manifest his dreaming body in the waking world, no matter how great a thing Milos and his friends seemed to think it was. He longed to stand on the beach in his bare feet, letting the incoming tide sift sand between his toes, connecting with good, solid earth.

Irrationally, he decided to try it.

He floated north a little ways until he came to a stretch of beach, and came to rest gently on wet sand, shining rivulets racing moonlight across the beach.

He looked at his feet, tried to imagine what they would look like without his boots, which nearly seemed a part of him these days.

At first nothing happened, but as he looked up again, at the line of waves crashing on the beach, he felt his feet dig into the sand. It wasn't quite the same...or was it?

He closed his eyes, frowned in concentration, holding the illusion of his body, and its coded responses to external stimuli, against the sound of the surf. He felt grains of sand against bare feet, felt the coldness of water, felt the wind against his bare arms.

He imagined how it would feel to be shirtless, and felt the biting wind whip at his naked torso. He looked down, half expecting to see that his shirt had regenerated, but he was indeed bare from the waist up. He laughed triumphantly and raised his hands to the sky, trying to draw down the wind, to whip up a storm...but the elements ignored him.

Feeling even the fleeting illusion of his own naked body was at once exultant and quite sad, for he knew it would pass unless he maintained an intensity of focus that would be quite impossible at this point. It was passing even now, the feeling moving elusively into the night. He was again but a dream, an apparition. He looked down. He was still barefoot, but his shirt had returned. It had gone from a rust color to dazzling white.

Far down the beach, a spot of moonlit silver-white drew his attention. He began moving towards it, floating slowly at first, then faster as he realized what it was. As he approached it, he slowed again until he was simply hovering over the sculpted sand of this forlorn, dream-lit beach.

All around, driftwood was scattered like the bleached bones of some ancient sea creature, dully reflecting the moonlight. Some of the larger pieces had collected drifts of sand on the windward side; the shadows cast in these hollows were dark and seemed somehow alive.

Jah-neee...!

The white raven sat majestically on a driftwood log, feathers gleaming under an iridescent moon. It looked bigger, more real, than he'd ever seen it, and he stared in wonder as it spread its wings, as if in greeting.

"What do you want from me?" His voice was strong, deliberate. He wasn't sure why he'd spoken aloud, as the thing had never spoken directly to him. Even its call, as it sounded again,

...Jah-neeeee...!

was a primal, animalistic sound, and he was sure that it was mostly his own imagination that likened the screeching cry to his own name. Still, he had a feeling it could understand him.

"You knew I would be here. Who are you?" He touched down, willing himself to feel the sand beneath his feet, suddenly needing to be grounded.

The night was a holy theater, a cathedral of magic in which only the two of them existed, the ocean a brilliant smear of blue-green under a phantom moon, lit as if from within, shot with streaks and auras of colors too many to name, purples and blues more lush than he'd ever seen.

He felt the sand; felt the wind; felt his whole body, suddenly, in a way he hadn't yet experienced. It was more real than real, more *there* than his physical body had ever been. He was a being of light, a net of etheric awareness, an electric presence, both giving and receiving. He felt something inside himself reach out, connecting with the entity before him who was not a bird; was not a woman; was like both, and yet unlike anything he knew.

A band of white-hot light roped from him toward the bird, a pulse of power that came from a place deep in the most secret garden of his mind, where grew all manner of wild and ravenous things.

The white raven responded, seeming to grow in his vision until it was half his height, wings spread, glowing and trembling.

It called again, loudly, sustaining the screech of its voice until it became something else, a pulsing tone that belled and fluted, carrying within it a wealth of emotional information. A flock of voices whispered his name in unison, and under that, other words formed, ululating in an exotic language he almost recognized but couldn't place. There was an ancient, unquenchable sadness there, a feeling too lost for words. It was sweet, almost palpable, a vibration in the very air.

A choice presented itself as he spun through the vortex that held the two of them. He knew his options instinctively, could feel her there, on the other side, waiting for the verdict.

He could withdraw...or he could allow it (*her*) to use his consciousness, his energy, like a ladder to pull itself (*herself*) from the nether regions where it (*she*) dwelled, to become

human

what it (*she*) wanted to be.

A terrible loneliness rose up in him, an anguish to match the sadness coming from the white raven. He wanted to pull back, to take time to think, but it seemed that the crushing weight of the universe suddenly rested squarely upon his imaginary shoulders.

The bird looked at him, its eyes communicating with him directly, sparking iridescent silver, large as two moons, and again he felt the tidal pull of ancient knowledge, the promise of secrets whispered in a dead tongue.

He hesitated, but only for a moment; the tide was simply too strong. He opened, and felt a mighty jolt, a flow like electricity as energy passed between the two of them.

The white raven began to change.

Its feathers began to fall off, one by one at first, then in clumps. Underneath, the skin rippled and glowed, pulsing with an insane light, again in too many shades of color to name. Violent shudders of ecstatic blue, yellow and orange light cascaded along its back, transforming the flesh beneath into something else.

Johnny could only watch, horrified yet fascinated.

Only its eyes remained the same now, luminous orbs locked with desperate intensity on his own, glittering preternaturally. The bird was gone, grown and twisted into something he couldn't yet recognize. His eyes tried to force the amorphous presence before him into alignment, tried to see its true form through a haze of shimmering color...

I have no form unless you give me form. Help me, Jah-nee. Help me.

The voice was soft, feminine, urgent. It rippled with an accent, an exotic overtone that he couldn't quite place. And those eyes...they were changing, finally, becoming a shade of green like a phosphor ocean on a distant planet. He saw things there, spirit visions that moved through his soul.

The eyes were only the beginning. Her face held him spellbound as he began to truly see her, the way he'd seen her the first time, when she'd appeared to him in the river. There was something fundamentally different this time, however. At the river, she'd seemed an apparition, a ghost rising from the water, somehow unfinished, unformed. Now she appeared real; more real by the second, in fact.

Dark, tangled hair fell around her face in windblown waves. Her skin was like polished white porcelain. Shadows emphasized the straightness of her nose, the fullness of her lips, the graceful lines of her shoulders. Her eyes were burning jade. She was naked, as she had been before, breasts full and soft in the moonlight, nipples dark and erect.

She took a step towards him, raised a trembling hand. He stood, transfixed. Her body was entire and complete, and lacking nothing in feminine beauty.

"Jah-nee," she said in a whisper. "I am here at last." She swallowed, her throat working convulsively. Her lips trembled. "I...thank you. You have...saved me." Her voice was exquisite, melodious and rich with an accent he couldn't place.

He couldn't take his eyes from her. Her body was voluptuous and soft, pale but inviting in the moonlight. He felt a stiffening in his groin, a hardness there he thought he'd forgotten how to feel. "Who are you?" He couldn't keep the amazement from his voice. Something about her was so familiar, so utterly harmonious, so...

She smiled and moved toward him, walking but seeming to float, as well. Her movements were graceful, almost liquid. She was the essence of silky femininity, and the reflex from his crotch quickened, real or not. A small groan escaped his lips.

The sense of super-reality persisted. He was a living array of primal awareness, a cohesion of energetic confluence that was no less human for being in a dream state.

Not a dream state. Not any more.

It was her voice, in his mind, with that same accent. He thought distractedly that it might be Indian, or maybe South American, but he couldn't tell.

She smiled, and her smile was beautiful and charming. "This is more than a dream-state. You are enhanced, Jah-nee. You are better than you were...more than you were. I know – I can feel your memories. What you call a dream state is but an arbitrary view from one point in the spectrum." She gestured with her hands to the surrounding night, the ecstatic roar of the ocean, the birds, the moonlight on the twisting, sculpted dunes. "Do not limit yourself. You can be whatever you want to be!"

His stare lingered on the soft curves of her belly, hips and thighs. She was a marvelous landscape of shadows in her own right, glistening under the ample swell of an engorged moon. She caught his gaze and laughed, a sound like tinkling bells.

From somewhere – he could not distinguish near from far – he heard and felt the *thump-THUMP, thump-THUMP* of his heart, pulsing through his veins a substance bloodier than blood.

She stroked the side of his face with the back of one of her soft, delicate hands, and the tingle that raced the length of his body was nothing if not real. He felt flushed, turned on in a way that was new to him, as so many things had surprised him since he'd become the dreamer. He looked down, and his body again felt like his own, in a way that was complete and then some. He was not too surprised to find that he was as naked as she was. His bare skin glowed a pale, cold white that matched hers. The wind was ice, but it did not cut. Rather it seemed to caress him, enhancing his state of arousal.

"We are the same," she whispered. "Dreamers caught in a dream."

His heart raced; his loins ached; her face was a monument, a tribute to a moment suspended in time. "You...you are a dreamer? Like me?"

"I don't know what I am," she said, twining her fingers through the hair at the nape of his neck, sending chills racing down his back. "But I know that I have been aware for...what you would call...millennia. I have been many things in many bodies. I have seen many wonders, and many horrors, on my journeys, but it is to this world that I am called, again and again. I believe it is my true home. I believe that I am human...or I was, once."

Her eyes clouded, pulled him in, a refugee from the storm that raged in his mind. A dizzying depth of eons lay behind those eyes, memories of cities and empires, suns gone nova.

"You have given me the energy I needed to become human again," she whispered into his ear, wrapping an arm around his neck, hand on his chest. Her touch was electric ice. "You are the only thing like myself that I have ever encountered, in all of my travels."

He couldn't speak. The night throbbed with possibilities.

"We are bound together," she said, floating behind him. Her breasts brushed against his back, somehow both warm and cold at the same time, nipples like the points of icicles. "Your energy sustains me," she whispered into his ear, "And I can teach you how to be what you want most."

"What do I want?" His voice was raw and husky.

She wrapped both arms around his neck, pressing herself against his back. "You want the same thing as me," she murmured. "You want to be human again. And I can show you how."

Her hands slid down his naked torso, across his belly and below. He groaned at her touch as she encountered the hardness there, gasped as she began to stroke it.

"How?!" he asked, his voice quavering, and gasped again at her electric touch. His body seemed to exude a white-heat glow. "How is this possible? I thought...I mean, I didn't know I could..."

"We are the same," she said again, her breath like a kitten's paw on the back of his neck and ears. "We are energy. We...*vibrate*...at the same rate. To each other, we are more real than real."

"But how?! I thought..."

"You think too much," she said. Her lips found the back of his neck, tongue flicking over his skin...real skin. His body was all there, solid and alive, more so than ever.

More so than ever.

Her hands quickened in their work, fingers stroking, probing. In his mind, it seemed he could hear again the lulling, breathless sing-song of words in an unknown language. She seemed all fingertips, lips and softness suddenly, massaging, kissing, pressing against him.

He turned to face her, pressing stiffly, almost painfully against her belly. Her eyes were dreamy, lips moist, mouth open slightly. He kissed her and she moaned softly.

His hand found its way down, across the mound of her belly and between her legs. The wetness his fingers encountered there was real too; impossibly real. He held her against his body, feeling the fullness, the softness of her, stroking her hair with one hand and her pubis with the other. Her eyes were globes of lust, dreaming.

"Look, Jah-nee," she murmured. "Look where we are."

They were floating, moving higher by the moment, slipping effortlessly into the sky with the wind and the clouds. The nightscape opened beneath them, the shoreline receding, a blue-black line in relief against the blue-green of the ocean. Overhead, the moon seemed impossibly close.

He laughed, feeling the buffeting wind against his naked thighs and buttocks. He ran his hands over her stomach and she spread for him. He entered her and she moaned deliriously, pushing back against him with an almost savage rocking motion.

"Jah-neee..." she breathed, holding his gaze. "We are one now, Jah-nee..."

Pleasure rocketed through him, and he exploded soundlessly, his mind seeming to disintegrate. Electric energy crackled along the lengths of his arms and legs. Her face spun before him, her jade eyes locked on his. White light encircled them, a tornado of energy that lit the night like fireworks. She cried out, mouth open, head thrown back...and then it seemed that the world had ended.

Overhead, the stars were like bright, ripe fruits, gazing fondly on the airborne lovers.

*****

Something had shifted. Everything was a shade of ethereal, blue-white light. Her eyes opened, focused on his. She smiled. "Thank you, Jah-nee," she said. "Your energy sustains me."

*****

The last throes of orgasm had fled, but still a strange energy sparked between them, a palpable, charged feeling. Johnny felt drowsy and light as a bubble. His eyes didn't seem to work very well, and he couldn't tell if the two of them were still entangled or not. His body, if it was still there, had retreated into the less-than-solid state that he'd gotten used to recently.

For an endless time it seemed that they floated like that, a single unit of energy, dreaming the void.

✳✳✳✳✳

Night was rolling up towards morning, the sky lightening in the east, above the mountains. In the west, the horizon was sullen with black clouds, brooding and intransigent. The threat of a storm hung in the air.

The moon was a ghost, low in the sky, her power usurped by the coming dawn.

They stood together, two dreamers in the dawnlight, atop the cliff that Johnny had come to and subsequently jumped from earlier that night. He looked down, again taking an inventory of their physical appearance, but it hadn't changed. He wore the same clothes as always; faded blue jeans, a rumpled brown shirt, his scuffed boots. No longer naked, she wore similar clothing; jeans, leather vest, light-colored shirt.

Johnny felt strong and light. He rose into the air, pirouetted once with his arms flung wide to the horizon, then landed next to her with feline grace. J'hara gazed at him, smiling, jade eyes alight. "You must make a choice, Jahnee," she said softly.

He met her gaze, unblinking. "What choice?"

"Whether you will stay with me, or go with the others," she said. Her eyes were haunted. "As much as I might like to, I will not coerce you. You must make this choice for yourself."

A solemn hush descended into the quiet cold. Johnny felt almost faint. "Where would we go?" His voice seemed to be coming from someplace far away.

She stroked his face with the smooth palm of one hand, and a furnace blast of delicious warmth washed through him, rocking him to his heels. She smiled. "To the city!" she said. "Where better to learn to be human?" She laughed quietly, a musical sound in the false twilight.

An awful anguish swept through Johnny; a sense of regret, of loss incomparable. "I have to help Maia," he whispered. "I can't...I mean, I *have* to...you understand? I have to help her. I'm the only one who can get her out."

A look of fright and pain passed across J'hara's face, a grimace that made her ugly for a moment. She took a deep breath and set her jaw. "I'll not compete for your attention," she said. "And I refuse to be what Milos has made me out to be. You deserve the right to choose your own path. But afterwards, what then, Jah-nee? I beg you to think about it."

"I will." Their eyes locked, and he felt the calm depths there, the perfect island of peace and rest in an ocean of chaos.

"We are well met," she said gravely. "We should not soon part, for I am of you, and you of me. We should stay together."

The feeling of faintness washed through him again, of being perfectly emptied, a receptacle. "I have to help Maia," he said again, stubbornly, holding onto that thought as if it could undo everything.

She nodded. Her eyes were luminous, reflecting an angry dawn. "I understand, Jah-nee. I will wait for you. Your energy will sustain me." She hesitated, biting at her lower lip. He watched her, fascinated. Her mannerisms were almost perfectly human, and becoming more so by the moment. Her eyes glimmered phosphor jade, and she smiled. "Until we meet again, then. I don't think I'll have to wait very long. This day brings an end to many things."

A bolt of light rent the air, a silent flash, and the white raven ascended on the wind, rising with the thermals, wheeling overhead. Her cry tore through the quietness of the morning.

Jah-neeee...! Jah-neeeeee...!

She wheeled again, huge and majestic, feathers fairly glowing. She seemed larger than ever, big as an eagle. He could almost feel the downdraft from her wings as they beat the air above his head once, twice...then she was gone, a white streak above the sea.

He stood in the ensuing silence, empty of thought, watching the dark horizon begin to lighten as the sun crept fearfully toward the tops of the peaks behind him.

He was pure reflection; an empty vessel, a lens to refract the light that was the essence of all things. Energy pooled in him, filling him from the bottoms of his feet to the top of his head, pulsing a primal rhythm, a pounding din. From somewhere – he could not distinguish near from far – he heard the *thump-THUMP, thump-THUMP* of his heart.

This day brings an end to many things.

"So be it," he said softly, to no one. He flexed his arms, bunching his hands into fists. "Let it be what it is."

He turned and began to walk back toward the camp, where Milos and company would surely soon be awake if they were not already. After a moment he lifted off, floating above the sawgrass, and disappeared among the twisted pines.

Below, the ocean continued to calmly pound the crumbling sand of the beach, as it had done for millions of years. Overhead, the sullen sky continued to brighten. In the west, the wall of thunderheads grew, dominating the horizon.

The wind began to blow.

The **Science** *of* Magic

Coming Soon

The **Dreaming** Fields:
Volume III

The Music of Perception

M.A. Wakefield

CHAPTER 1

Simon DaLuge awoke uneasily, drawn from restless dreams toward the gloomy first light of an overcast day. Premature spatters of rain specked the single window of his bedroom. His thoughts were scattered, but the pulse of destiny throbbed in his veins. His eyes snapped open as his mind circled, honing in, gaining focus.

It's that day, Simon. Biggest day of your life.

He sighed and sat up on his narrow bed, reaching for his glasses.

He didn't know exactly what it was that was making him so uneasy. All systems had been checked and re-checked; the motherboard was functioning at full capacity, the REMdrive was fully charged, and all backup cells as well; and the electric suit had surpassed all expectations in the final simulations. Daniel's body had responded indifferently to the tissue sample he'd been injected with, and though they had run out of time for more extensive testing, DaLuge was almost entirely convinced that the suit would perform admirably.

But something was wrong.

Something about the clone?

The evening after his physical, Daniel had suffered a bit of a collapse; a nervous breakdown, in DaLuge's expert opinion. He'd examined Daniel that night, lying unconscious on a white-sheeted table in his lab, with Randall's steely gaze assessing from his chair in the corner of the room, and concluded that there was no real problem. Daniel seemed to be suffering from exhaustion, but his body's systems were normal, including his brain and synaptic responses.

Still, it didn't bode well. Lazaro Sol had insisted upon keeping the boy unconscious for the past two days, which DaLuge didn't like too much. He'd administered the last of the sleeping drugs late the previous night himself, keeping the dosage low.

As he checked the chronometer next to the com-unit on his desk, he saw that the clone should be awakening before too long now.

We should never have activated him early. That was Lazaro Sol's paranoia.

The truth did little to dispel his rancor.

It doesn't matter who did it. It should never have happened. The problem was with the imaging generators, and I've fixed that. It was never the mother program.

He pulled his robe over his shoulders, slid his feet into his slippers and stood up, feeling shaky and disoriented. He picked up the glass of water on his nightstand and chased down two caffeine pills, then retrieved his silver cigarette-case and put one of the smooth white cylinders to his lips.

He didn't light it at first, just stood, swaying a bit, beside his bed.

So this is what it comes to, then? Smoking first thing in the morning? Gods! I must really be stressed out.

He laughed bitterly and reached into the pocket of his terrycloth robe, extracting an old-fashioned silver cigarette lighter. He took another drink from the glass, set it back down, then immediately reconsidered and took it with him out to his patio, which faced the ponderous, imminent slopes of the mountains to the east, heavy with dew and the promise of more precipitation.

He snapped open the lighter and lit the cigarette, relishing the tang of smoke as it rolled over his tongue, enjoying the drizzle of rain and the gusting wind as it blew his unkempt hair about his face.

How long since I've even been out here?

He didn't know. He'd been sleeping on the cot in his semi-private office for weeks on end, only returning to his quarters occasionally for a change of clothes, a shower, or - like last night - when he was simply too exhausted to continue without a real night's sleep.

He took another deep drag, jetted fragrant smoke into the crisp morning air, his malaise reduced to a single question.

Have I missed something?

He sighed, tapped ash into the gusting breeze.

No way to tell.

There were simply too many variables, and no way of knowing until it was done. And, for better or worse, it was going to happen.

It was going to happen today.

About The Author

Matt Wakefield currently resides in the Pacific Northwest with his longtime partner and their menagerie of docile animals (including some offspring).

OMINOUS PRODUCTIONS
2020